DAY OF AWAKENING

The Beginning

Jessica Baker

CONTENTS

Title Page	1
Introduction	5
Chapter 1	7
Chapter 2	17
Chapter 3	36
Chapter 4	40
Chapter 5	55
Chapter 6	78
Chapter 7	98

© **Copyright 2019 - All rights reserved.**
The contents of this book may not be reproduced, duplicated or transmitted without direct written permission from the author.

Under no circumstances will any legal responsibility or blame be held against the publisher for any reparation, damages, or monetary loss due to the information herein, either directly or indirectly.

Legal Notice:
This book is copyright protected. This is only for personal use. You cannot amend, distribute, sell, use, quote or paraphrase any part or the content within this book without the consent of the author.

Disclaimer Notice:
Please note the information contained within this document is for educational and entertainment purposes only. Every attempt has been made to provide accurate, up to date and reliable complete information. No warranties of any kind are expressed or implied. Readers acknowledge that the author is not engaging in the rendering of legal, financial, medical or professional advice. The content of this book has been derived from various sources. Please consult a licensed professional before attempting any techniques outlined in this book.

By reading this document, the reader agrees that under no circumstances are is the author responsible for any losses, direct or indirect, which are incurred as a result of the use of information contained within this document, including, but not limited to, —errors, omissions, or inaccuracies.

INTRODUCTION

In the middle of July, when the sun is hot enough to cast heat waves over the asphalt, a woman has lost her mind in the small town of Lynden, Washington. She is intent on one thing: consuming living flesh. Her hunger cannot be satisfied, and it spreads like a disease, sweeping through the town and ripping it apart. The air is full of the sounds of screams, the stench of blood, and something else. Something foreign. Something that is at work but cannot be seen.

Violet, a young bartender, is determined to escape the chaos that has suddenly been let loose in Lynden. She must make it to Seattle to find her mother and sister. They need her, and with communications down there is no way for her to get in touch with them to find out if they are alright- or even alive. Violet knows that she must do everything in her power to find her family. They are all she has left, and she can't allow them to meet a slow death at the hands of merciless crazed cannibals.

Fynn, Lynden's most dangerous and misunderstood young man who drowns memories of his dark past in alcohol, decides to join Violet on her mission to Seattle. He is not her first choice for company, but with people ripping each other to pieces, Violet takes comfort in the simple fact that she is not alone. Fynn may be her least favorite person in Lynden, but he has a mean right hook and an uncanny ability for getting himself out of trouble. Together, they find themselves in a bloody battle for survival. It is a battle they soon realize they are not prepared for.

This is the Apocalypse.

Will the rise of the living dead be enough to force Violet and Fynn to work together? Nobody can survive alone. Perhaps a night on a rooftop under the stars will be enough to unite the two of them. If they can put their differences aside they just might be able to make it to Seattle alive... but will there be anything left to find there, or will the reckoning have already sunk its bloody fingers into the belly of the city, leaving nothing behind but bodies and fire?

CHAPTER 1

I dragged my beer stained rag across the surface of the cherry oak bar before tucking it into the back pocket of my jeans. The clock on the wall above the pool tables told me that it was only five in the evening. I still had seven hours of my shift left to go, and I was already sick and tired of picking up broken peanut shells and wiping away alcohol spills. I put my hands on my hips and sighed at the ceiling. Only seven more hours until I could enjoy the sunny evening of July 14th on my Apartment's patio- maybe with a glass of chilled white wine in hand while I buried my nose in my book.

A familiar freckled face wove through the crowded bar to stand in front of me. Cassidy, my oldest friend, rested both her elbows on the bar and waggled her red eyebrows at me.

"Hey Vi," she chimed, "your manager here today?"

"No," I said, already anticipating her next question.

"Wanna hook me up with a free drink or two?"

I chuckled, poured her favourite drink- a concoction of rum, soda, and a splash of cherry for sweetness- and slid it across the bar to her. "Put whatever extra change you have in your wallet in my tip jar and we'll be square."

Cassidy rolled her eyes but obliged. She fished out a collection of six quarters and dropped them in the mason jar on the counter labeled 'pity money'. I had a sense of humor sometimes. Unfortunately, it wasn't appreciated by all the bar's customers, and Cassidy's tip brought my total earnings for the day to a nice whopping six dollars. The afternoon shift was the worst. No one was drunk enough to tip decently, regardless of how flirty my smile was.

She slid to the side to make way for other patrons who might want to order a drink and made herself comfortable on one of the red fabric lined barstools. She rested her cheek in her hand and blew a strand of curly red hair off her face. "So," she said happily, "how's life treating the small town bartender today?"

I shrugged a shoulder and leaned one hip against the bar. "Oh, things are just lovely. I've already spilled a beer on my jeans and burned my knuckle on the deep fryer in the kitchen. And, of course, I spent the first forty minutes of my shift entertaining Fynn. I don't understand why he's *always* here." I took the rag out of my back pocket and mindlessly began wiping the bar down again.

"Um, because this place has the cheapest drinks in Lynden."

"Right," I said, "he just makes me so... uneasy."

"It's the eyes," Cassidy said knowingly as she stirred her drink with her straw. "It's like he's looking right through you. Or into you. I'm rambling. Nevermind."

I looked over Cassidy's shoulder to the table in the far corner. Fynn was sitting there, as per usual, with his hands in the front pockets of his black sweatshirt. The scowl he wore was the same one I had seen on his dark features every day for the last couple of years. His bad attitude matched his sour outward appearance. He lifted his beer to his lips and drained half the bottle in three easy mouthfuls. I groaned inwardly, knowing he would be returning to the bar to order another one within the next five minutes or so.

"How was work?" I asked Cassidy in an attempt to distract myself.

"Good," she said. Cassidy worked as a pharmacy assistant at the drugstore down the road. She fished the maraschino cherry out of the bottom of her glass and popped it in her mouth. "I'm glad it's the weekend. Supposed to be hot as hell. You up for a day at the beach?"

"Always," I said, my eyes returning to Fynn in the background as he stumbled to his feet and started staggering over to us. Cassidy must have sensed the change in my mood because she stiffened on her stool and glanced over her shoulder.

Fynn leaned up against the bar beside her for support. His dark brown eyes swept back and forth between us, and a lazy smile pressed dimples into his cheeks. "Ladies," he slurred.

Cassidy offered him a polite nod while I popped the cap off another beer and passed it to him. He seized it by the neck, lifted it in the air as a way of saying thanks, and took a sip. He shifted around so that his back was to me and rested his elbows behind him on the bar.

Cassidy was distracting herself by rattling her ice cubes around her now empty glass. I took it away from her and made her another drink. As I dropped the ounce of rum into the glass I watched Fynn's back.

It was no secret in Lynden that Fynn had spent time in jail for fighting. He had a reputation in the small town for his temper and his fists, which I had seen in action only once- and it was enough.

"Hey Vi," Cassidy said, distracting me from my thoughts, "turn up the TV will you? The news was on all day at work. Some weird stuff going on."

Thankful for the distraction, I stretched on to my tiptoes and turned up the volume on the television set. Somebody had stolen our remote over a year ago, and the owner of the bar was too cheap to purchase a new one.

I backed up a pace and crossed my arms over my chest while I tuned out all the background noise around me. The female reporter on the screen stood in front of a smoky city skyline. I realized quite suddenly that it was New York City.

"*Riots have broken out in Time Square,*" the reporter said. "*People are swarming the streets after an increase in aggression over the last couple of days. Police say they received ten times the amount of domestic violence calls in the last three days than normal. Most calls ended with the victim in hospital, or, in a few cases, dead. The riot teams are down on the ground now trying to control the situation, and we are not allowed past the city limits. We will keep you posted as time goes on."*

"That's crazy," Cassidy breathed behind me. "Ten times the amount of domestic violence calls? What's in the water in New York?"

"Water?" Fynn scoffed, finishing the rest of his beer. He was facing me again and had his body draped lazily against the bar.

Cassidy raised a disapproving eyebrow. "Yes, water. Some of us still drink that, you know. Wouldn't be so bad if you treated yourself to some good old fashioned H2O every now and then. I'm sure your liver would thank you for it."

Fynn rolled his eyes at her then turned his gaze on me. His hawkish stare wasn't nearly as intense as it usually was- the copious amounts of beer he had consumed in the last hour had seen to that. I scooped some ice into a glass and topped it up with water. When I slid it over to him he scowled at me.

He looked at it like I was trying to poison him. Finally he wrapped his fingers around the glass and lifted it to his mouth. I watched his bottom lip as it pressed against the rim of the glass. The stubble on his jaw distracted me, and I caught myself admiring the sharp lines of his face.

Before he took a sip the doors to the bar burst open. Three men with wide and wild eyes stumbled in. One, a man I knew from the hardware store around the corner as Harry, looked around anxiously, grabbed a chair, and broke one of the legs off over his thigh. Patrons were backing away from them as the other two men slammed the doors closed. One of my coworkers, Alicia, started loudly scolding Harry for breaking one of the chairs. The men at the doors called for the broken chair leg and slid it through both door handles. They locked the doors and all three men backed away.

The door suddenly shuddered under the weight of something outside. Something that wanted to get in.

I jumped and yelped when Fynn slammed his water glass on the bar. It shattered, sending glass and ice fell to the floor. "What the hell is going on?" He demanded, putting his back to me and facing the three men.

Harry looked back at us. I could see beads of sweat on his forehead. Then I noticed the blood staining the forearm of his jacket. "People are losing it out there," he said quietly. "A guy came into my shop to buy some tools. When I was ringing him through he went mental. He… he bit me. I got away from him and when I made it outside everyone was freaking out."

"He bit you?" Fynn asked, his tone implying that he thought Harry had lost his mind.

Harry held up his bloody arm. "Took a decent chunk out of me too. I'm not the only one. A couple others on the street… we can't go outside. Somebody help me board up the windows."

Nobody seemed willing to comply with his request. We all stared at him stupidly as the jukebox in the corner blasted out a rock tune from the eighties. Harry snapped into action, and he and his friends began drawing the curtains closed on all the windows.

Cassidy turned to me. "Uh, what the fuck?"

"What the fuck is right," Fynn said, his eyes following the men as they ushered people out of their tables and away from the windows. "They've lost it."

I glanced behind me at the television. "Or whatever is happening in New York is happening here too."

Fynn cast me a glance over his shoulder. "How 'bout a beer on the house?"

"Sorry," I growled, "the bar is closed."

There was an ear-splitting thunderous crack followed by somebody screaming.

Fynn whirled around and I stared past him at the front doors, which had blown inwards. Through them came several people who walked with strange, crooked gaits. One of them, a woman in a pale yellow sundress, cocked her head to the side and observed all of us. We stared back. Her lips parted and her mouth opened wide- wide enough that for a moment I thought her jaw must be broken. A wail of sound came out of her. The others who had come in with her started shrieking as well. The sound was a vicious attack on my ears. I slapped my hands over them and gritted my teeth against it.

My stomach leapt into my throat when the woman in yellow raced forward. Her mouth was still hanging open and her arms were stretched out in front of her. She got hold of an older man in a plaid shirt and hauled him towards her. He struggled in her grip, but his efforts to break free of her were useless. Her wide mouth pressed against his neck, and then, with a snapping sound, it clamped shut.

Blood leaked out of the man's neck and stained the woman's dress. She wriggled her head back and forth until a chunk of flesh tore off of her victim's neck. The man fell to his knees at her feet and pressed a hand over the wound. Blood pumped out between his fingers and raced down his forearm. The man's wife rushed forward and grabbed hold of his shoulders. Her panicky voice was drowned out by the screaming of the others.

The woman in the yellow dress pushed the strip of skin and muscle into her mouth with her thumb and swallowed without chewing. Her mouth dropped open again and she turned to Harry. She charged him and he hurried backwards until his back hit the wall. She smothered him. He knocked her down. She crumpled in front of him but hauled herself back up by grabbing hold of the waist of his jeans. That gaping mouth of hers found the soft skin of his belly. Before I knew what was happening, she had taken a bite out of him that was big enough to make him scream bloody murder.

The whole bar erupted with panic. I stumbled backwards until my back hit the liquor shelf. Cassidy jumped down off her barstool and raced through the opening along the bar for employees. "We have to get out of here!" She shouted as she passed me. She grabbed me by the wrist and pulled me along behind her through the swinging kitchen doors.

Some of the cooks were scrambling by us to see what all

the commotion was out front. I looked back as they blew out through the saloon style doors. All I could see were blood stained curtains and wide open mouths. I shook my head and turned back to Cassidy, who was still pushing forward. Her fingers on my wrist were incredibly tight.

We rounded a corner and took to the stairs that led up to the second story where the offices and breakroom was. A voice called my name and I spotted Kent, our young dishwasher, standing with a towel slung over his shoulder at the bottom of the stairs.

"Come on!" I screamed at him.

He was frozen in place and watching us as we continued to climb. Then someone dressed in black slammed into his back and he pitched forward, catching himself on the bottom stair.

Fynn had arrived in an unorganized jumble of drunken limbs. He grabbed Kent by the back of the shirt and hauled him to his feet before shoving him up the stairs. "Get a move on, kid!" He shouted, and the two of them followed us up.

We rounded the corner at the top and hurried into the breakroom. Cassidy went to the window with Fynn hot on her heels. Together they wedged it open and peered out.

"What's going on guys?" Kent asked timidly.

"Later," I breathed, going to the window. I rested my hands on the sill and peered down at the alley below. Right beneath the window was a pile of trash bags.

"Time to go," Fynn said as he pushed me out of the way and put his foot on the edge. Then he climbed out, gave us a devil-may-care grin, and jumped.

I blinked at the window for a moment before I gathered my wits and stuck my head out. Fynn was climbing his way out of the trash bags. He looked up at us and gave us thumbs up. He then turned his head on a swivel, looking back and forth down the alley. He looked back up at us and mouthed, *'hurry up'*.

Cassidy went next. I steadied her by the elbow as she balanced herself on the ledge. She let out a weak whimper before she let herself fall. I climbed out after her and waited for her to be clear of the garbage before I let go of the window frame. Wind rushed in my ears for half a second, and then my nose was filled with the stench of rotting, moldy food.

I clambered free of the garbage bags and brushed pieces of lettuce and peanut shells off my jeans. I looked up in time to see the young dishwasher emerging from the window. He didn't hesitate. He let himself fall and landed heavily in the garbage. "I'm alright," he said as he sifted his way out of the garbage pile; a hint of surprise coloring his tone.

"Now what?" Cassidy interrupted.

"My place isn't far," I suggested.

"Neither is mine," Kent offered, looking between all of us as if waiting for someone else to call the shots or offer up another solution. Cassidy and Fynn weren't forthcoming with offers to go to their places. Cassidy lived on the other side of town. It didn't make sense to go there. And Fynn- I didn't know where Fynn lived, but I couldn't see it as a logical place to go right now.

"I imagine Violet has a better stocked fridge. We might need supplies," Fynn said, a hint of impatience coloring his voice.

Kent shrugged his shoulders and nodded in my direction. "He's probably right."

I wrung my hands anxiously. "Okay. My place it is then."

Cassidy nodded beside me and grabbed my hands. She gave my fingers a warm, somewhat sweaty squeeze.

We tread quietly down the alley until we reached the main street. Fynn poked his head out while he kept himself pressed up against the alley wall. He looked back at us. I could hear the commotion out there and I could see in Fynn's eyes that the street was just as bad as the bar.

"If we can cut across the road and make it to the alley on the other side," Fynn said evenly, "we can cut through Watson's Park. Then it's a straight shot down the back alley behind your apartments, right Violet?"

"Yeah, basically." Right now felt like an inappropriate time to ask Fynn how he knew where I lived- and pointless. Had people not just started eating each other, I would have confronted him about it.

Fynn nodded and looked back out at the street. "Alright, when I say go, we run for it. As fast as you can. Clear?"

We all nodded in unison.

Fynn's knuckles were white as he braced himself against the wall. I waited, anxiety building in my chest and blood rushing in my ears. When Fynn shouted for us to run my legs suddenly felt like they were made of lead. Kent and Cassidy blew by me and I managed to put one foot in front of the other.

Out on the street my senses were bombarded. It smelled like smoke, copper, and burnt meat. Cars were upside down and on their sides all over the place. The pavement was decorated in shattered glass and blood. A lot of blood. Fynn ran through a puddle of it and left bloody boot prints in his wake for the rest of us to follow. People were screaming and others were crying. Some were calling out names of friends and loved ones.

What I noticed above all was a young girl, no more than twelve, leaning over a body in the middle of the street. At first I thought she was crying. She was bowed so low over the corpse that it seemed as if she was pressing her forehead against its stomach. I slowed down and veered left to go to her.

Somebody grabbed my upper arm and yanked me forwards. Their grip was firm and promised a decent bruise. I tried to squirm away but they held me fast. I looked up to find Fynn's angry glare on me.

"Keep moving," he said loudly over the screaming, "it's not what you think."

He pulled me along and I looked back at the girl. "We can't leave her here!" I shouted, but Fynn didn't let go of me.

The little girl heard me yelling and she lifted her face. I felt sweat bloom to life on my skin. My stomach rolled and a lump formed in my throat that made it hard to breathe.

The girl's eyes were pale and fixed on me. The stare she studied me with was hollow and empty. Her mouth and nose were stained in blood. Her hands were buried in the guts of the person lying on the road in front of her. She lifted one hand, and long sinewy strands of red were wrapped around her fingers. She promptly tilted her head back and shook the gore into her mouth. Loose strands slapped against her throat and left thin snaking stains in their wake. It made it look like she had a red octopus stretching its tentacles out of her open mouth in a desperate attempt for freedom.

She vanished from sight when Fynn dragged me into the alley. He didn't let go of me as we continued to run straight through to the other side. We emerged on a much quieter street and made straight for Watson's park. The gravel of the path crunched under my boots as we wove through it, slowing to a light jog when we were under the cover of trees.

None of us said a word. We pushed ahead and Fynn finally released my arm. He took the lead and I brought up the rear. I looked backwards every ten or so steps to make sure no one- or no *thing*- was following us.

We were alone.

CHAPTER 2

I fumbled with my keys in my front door for a solid thirty seconds before I finally managed to stop the shaking in my hands long enough to slide the key in the deadbolt. I pushed the door open and we all rushed inside. I shut the door and locked the deadbolt and handle. I turned to face the others and pressed my shoulder blades up against the door.

My knees were shaking with nerves as I watched the others make their way into my home. The place was a stark contrast to the chaos and gore outside. The old scratched up hardwood floors were covered with haphazardly scattered carpets of a variety of colors and patterns- I had picked most of them up at local flea markets. My book shelves lined the south wall and were wrapped in warm white twinkle lights. This was the only light illuminating the place, and it cast everything into a pleasant, warm glow.

"Turn the T.V. on," Cassidy said to Fynn, who had wandered aimlessly into the middle of my living room.

He dropped down on to my sofa and plucked the remote from my coffee table. He turned on the television and the screen glowed a bright blue. He began flicking through the channels. Each one showed the same brilliant blue screen.

Fynn stood and with an angry shout he hurled the remote across the room. It smashed into one of my bookshelves. He ran his fingers through his messy dark hair before collapsing back on the sofa.

"What does that mean?" Kent asked.

"I don't know," I said, padding into my kitchen and turning on the radio. It offered nothing but static. "What do we do?"

Cassidy went to my window in the living room and peered outside. "It's a nightmare out there," she breathed, drawing my curtain- a bohemian patterned blanket- further aside to get a better look. She let the curtain fall and turned back to the rest of us. Her eyes were glassy. "We can't be out there at night... people are still... they're still eating."

"My mom and my sister are in Seattle," I said, trying to deviate the conversation away from the cannibalism taking place out on the street. "Does anyone have a cell phone? Mine has no signal."

Cassidy fished hers out of her pocket and handed it to me. I pressed the home button. "No service," I groaned. "Of course. What is going on?"

"It's like a horror movie," Kent said, joining Fynn on the sofa. "It's like a really messed up, real, Goddamn horror movie."

I pressed the heels of my hands against my eyes. My little sister Addison was only eleven. She and my mother had moved to Seattle the previous year when my mom landed a full time nursing position at the hospital. I had stayed behind in an attempt to forge my own path. A year later I was still working at the same dead end job. "I need to get to my mom," I said. "You guys can stay here. I don't care. But I'm going to try to take a train to-"

"Are you crazy?" Cassidy asked, planting her fists on her hips. "Did you not see what was happening out there? You can't go on your own, especially not right now."

"Well what am I supposed to do?" I pleaded, hearing the desperation in my voice.

Cassidy let her arms fall to her sides as tears welled in my eyes. "Wait until morning," she said eventually. "Wait until morning, and I'll go with you."

"What?"

"We can leave as early as you like. But going out there right now... that's insane. Will you wait?" She rested a reassuring hand on my shoulder and gave it a gentle squeeze. "Things will be clearer in the morning. Does anyone have a car?" She turned to the others as she addressed the room.

"No," Kent and Fynn said in unison. Neither Cassidy or I had our own vehicles either. Lynden was a small place, and a car was unnecessary. I was regretting my choice not to purchase an old yellow hatchback I had happened across in the spring.

"I can always get us a car relatively easily," Fynn offered, once shoulder inching towards his ear in a weak shrug.

I licked my lips. Morning was far away. There was a lot that could change overnight. Things could get worse; things could get much worse. Or they could get better. Whatever this was might be temporary. Maybe by morning the television stations would be back up and running and we would have information about what we were supposed to do- or where we were supposed to go. A car would take time to find with all the chaos on the streets, and it would take even longer to get it started without keys. "Morning," I nodded. "I can wait until morning. But if we don't have a car.." I trailed off, hoping someone else might have a better idea.

"Things might be different in the city," Kent said hopefully. "The Seattle Police Department and the military won't be idly standing by if people are attacking each other. It could be safer there. It could also be like New York. Things there looked bad." He stopped talking when he realized his words were creating an even thicker tension in the room. He shook his head as if to shake away the negative thoughts and lifted his gaze to me. "I'll join you. Take the train. Straight shot into downtown Seattle. It's faster than a car by a long shot."

I glanced at Fynn who now had his arms draped over the back of my sofa. He met my gaze and his eyebrows inched up towards his hairline. "What?" He asked defensively.

"Are you going to stay here?" I asked.

"Is that an invitation?" He said.

"Sure," I said, glancing at Cassidy. She nodded encouragingly. Having another guy with us wouldn't be a bad thing- especially one that was known for having a mean right hook.

Fynn buried his hand in the pocket of his sweater and

pulled out a bottle of whiskey. "Well, now that we've settled on a plan," he said mischievously as he unscrewed the cap, "who's thirsty?" He pressed it to his lips and took a sip before handing it to Kent.

Kent smelled it and recoiled. "That's disgusting."

"Tastes even worse," Cassidy said as she walked around the front of the sofa and sat on the floor in front of them. She patted the ground beside her and nodded at me. I joined them and Cassidy took the whiskey from Kent. She drank four easy mouthfuls and handed it to me.

Several thoughts ran through my head.

I had just seen a little girl eating someone in the middle of the road. People were losing their minds. There were riots on the street. The bar was in shambles. My mother and sister were somewhere in the big city on their own. Drinking seemed like a terrible idea.

Not drinking seemed worse.

I matched Cassidy's four mouthfuls. Kent took a swig and wiped his mouth with the back of his hand. Then, for the next hour or so, we passed the bottle around.

When it was gone I rummaged through my cupboards and found a bottle of wine. We shared that and Kent promptly passed out on the sofa with his hand cupped under his cheek. Cassidy was quick to follow. She curled herself up in my arm chair in the far corner and covered her legs with one of my fleece blankets. Kent's snores filled the room and Fynn and I found ourselves sitting on the floor sipping cheap wine and listening to the sounds of car alarms wailing outside.

"Never thought I'd get to see the inside of Violet Morgan's place," Fynn said thickly, casting his gaze around my living room. "It's exactly what I expected."

"Really?" I asked dryly.

"Really. Cozy blankets everywhere. Lots of books. Yellow walls. It's you in a nutshell."

"You don't even know me. The only time we ever talk is when you order a drink. Even then, you barely say a word. You grunt the word 'beer' and that's about it."

"Why waste unnecessary words?" Fynn said. The smile on his lips looked forced. He looked down at his lap and began picking at a loose thread on his jeans. I noticed the shadows his eyelashes cast on his cheeks. He was, and always had been, quite handsome.

"You don't have to come to the city with us tomorrow if you don't want to," I said suddenly, surprising myself by offering him a way out.

He looked up from his jeans. That piercing dark stare held me in place for several moments. When he spoke he took his time- he was choosing his words carefully. "Hanging back here won't do me any favors."

I bit my bottom lip and looked everywhere but at him. "Is there anyone you should bring with us? We can check your place before we go-"

"There's no one," he said bluntly.

"Oh."

Silence hung between us for an agonizingly uncomfortable minute. Wine sloshed gently in the bottle as Fynn took another sip. "It doesn't matter," he said finally. "Not having anyone to worry about is a blessing right now."

I thought of my mother. Of my little sister. I didn't think he had meant for his words to sound cruel, but I couldn't help but feel a pang of misery and hopelessness in my gut. "It couldn't have been a blessing for the last twenty something years," I said.

"It's a matter of perspective, I suppose."

"What does that mean?"

He returned to picking at the thread on his jeans. I crossed my legs under myself and waited for him to explain himself. After a while I realized that he had no intention of doing so. He took another drink of wine and handed me the bottle. As I took a sip he settled himself down on my area rug. He knit his hands behind his head to use them as a pillow, and once he was comfortable he closed his eyes.

I watched him for a while. It didn't take long for his breathing to even out. Sleep had settled in and erased his permanent scowl. He was peaceful, in sleep, and I found my gaze wandering from the cut of his jaw to the tanned skin showing at the hem of his sweatshirt above the waist of his jeans. Working as a roofer all summer had done him some favors. It had also fattened his wallet with enough bills to drink himself stupid several nights a week.

I sighed and grabbed the throw pillow at Kent's feet. I fluffed it up and settled down on the floor. My shoulder blades dug into the ground. The discomfort wasn't enough to keep me awake. The alcohol had made me tired and groggy. Not even the sound of the car alarms outside disrupted the calm that washed over me and wrapped me up in comforting arms.

The blaring racket of the car alarms outside were silent when I woke in the morning. The pale gray light that was seeping through my windows told me it wasn't even dawn yet. I suspected it was between five or six in the morning. I fished my phone out of the back pocket of my jeans. The screen brightened at my touch and confirmed my suspicions. It was half past five, and there was still no phone signal. I sighed, reached my hands above my head and stretched my spine. My back cracked and my shoulder blades pressed into the hardwood floor.

I rolled on to my side and got to my feet. My stomach gave a sickening lurch and my head spun. The whiskey and the wine had, in retrospect, been a terrible idea.

Kent was still sleeping on the couch. His back was to me as he snored softly. Cassidy was still asleep in my armchair in the far corner. Fynn, however, was gone.

I padded to the kitchen to find him rummaging through my drawers and peering in cupboards. I leaned against the doorframe and crossed my arms. "Something I can help you find?" I asked, my tongue feeling thick and dry in my mouth.

Fynn didn't so much as look over his shoulder. He went to my fridge, yanked it open, and began pulling out all the water bottles I had in the door. He was cramming them into a backpack- one of mine, I realized. So he had gone through my closets, too.

"It's hot out there," Fynn said finally, "and I don't want to make any unnecessary stops. Is that a problem?"

"No," I scowled. "You could have asked first."

He dropped the last water bottle in the bag. As he zipped it up he gave me an irritated once over. "You should change."

I looked down at my jeans and sandals. "What's wrong with this?"

"Don't you have something more practical? Sneakers? Anything?"

"Well, yes, I guess-"

Fynn shrugged the backpack over his shoulder. "It's your call. If you want to make the trip to Seattle dressed like that, be my guest. But don't be whining in my ear when your feet hurt. Do you have any more bags?"

I opened my mouth to argue and realized that I didn't have a rebuttal worth my breath. He was right. Trekking to the city in form fitting name brand denim wouldn't be the most comfortable thing- neither would my plastic bedazzled sandals. I chewed the inside of my cheek for a moment longer before going to the closet in my bedroom. I found an extra backpack and changed into a pair of hiking shorts, running shoes, and a white tank top. I grabbed a similar ensemble for Cassidy to put on before we left. Then I returned to Fynn and handed him the other bag.

He began filling it with more of my stuff: granola bars, apples, bananas, and bread. He told me to grab a sweater, just in case we found ourselves somewhere cold. I found a plaid one hanging by my front door and tied it around my waist.

"Are you one of those crazy preppers?" I asked.

Fynn zipped up the second backpack and dropped it by the front door. "A prepper?"

"You know, one of those guys who buys a lot of guns and has a bomb shelter filled with sardines and spam? In case the world ends?"

"No," Fynn said, the faintest hint of a smile curling the corner of his mouth. He tugged his black sweater off over his head. The gray shirt he wore underneath got caught up around his navel and he pulled it hastily down. I still got a good look at his muscular stomach and a pale pink scar across his right hip that vanished beneath the waistband of his jeans. "Go wake the others, we should get going."

Cassidy was in a sour mood when I shook her awake. I gave her the change of clothes I had picked out and told her to hurry and change. I could hear her grumbling in my bedroom as she shimmied into the shorts and top. Kent woke with a yawn but sat up rather bright eyed. He took one of the bags from Fynn and hoisted it over his shoulder.

"So, to the train?" Kent asked. "On foot it won't take us long to get there. Fifteen minutes at the most. Ten if we really hustle. We should keep to the back roads. Take Lincoln up to Dawson, and then it's a straight shot to the station. Stay away from the main roads. Away from people."

Fynn went to the window and pulled my curtain-blanket back. I watched the back of his head as he peered up and down the street. "There's nobody out there," he said, turning back to us.

"Good," I said, "you're sure the train is the fastest way into Seattle, right?"

"As far as I know," Kent said with a mild shrug and dubious eyebrow raise. "The only hold up is if we run into any of those nutjobs out there."

"Like I said, it looks pretty quiet," Fynn said lazily. "Besides, we don't have much of a choice."

"Do you need to go home first?" I asked Kent as butterflies began swarming my stomach with nerves. "Is there anyone there who might need help?"

"Nope," Kent said nonchalantly.

"Really? You're sure you don't-"

"I'm sure," he said, silencing me with a quick sharp stare.

I swallowed and felt my cheeks burn. Then I cast one longing glance around my living room. It might be a while before I ever set foot back in my home. Thoughts of my mother and sister chased away the homesickness that was already stirring inside me. "Let's go," I said.

Fynn took the lead. We followed him out my front door

and on to the street, where we all cast nervous looks left and right before taking to the sidewalk.

The place was like a ghost town.

I swallowed the uneasiness that was clawing to get out of my chest and continued putting one foot in front of the other. Cassidy walked along beside me. We pressed ourselves up against each other for comfort, our hips and elbows and shoulders bumping continuously against one another. At any other time I would have told her to give me space. I would have found it annoying. Now I didn't dare say a word. If I could have welded our bodies together, I would have.

Kent walked behind us and checked over his shoulder frequently to make sure nothing was coming up behind us. We persevered, keeping to side streets and alleys and avoiding the main roads at all costs.

My eyes caught movement up ahead. Someone was crossing the street. I didn't realize that I had stopped walking. All of us watched as the stranger- an older man in coveralls that were spattered in blood- staggered over the dotted line in the middle of the road. He stared unseeing at his feet as he moved and his body swayed from left to right as if he had been caught in a strong gust of wind.

On the other side of the street he stepped on to the curb and continued walking until his face was pressed up against the glass of the local book store. It took him at least thirty seconds to conclude that he couldn't walk through the glass. He turned left and continued shuffling down the sidewalk.

Up a couple more blocks was another man decorated in blood spatters. His arms were bare and appeared to be too thin for his body. As he drew closer I could see that the flesh on his forearms had been torn away, revealing bone and gore and making him look like a gangly corpse.

Fynn ducked to his right and we followed him between two buildings. I grabbed his shoulder. "What the hell are these things?"

He peered around the corner and talked to us over his

shoulder. "They have injuries that would have made them bleed out, but they're still standing somehow." He was stating the obvious. "We're going to have to keep to the alleys. Hide behind parked cars if we have to take the main roads. We don't need these things getting any ideas and trying to follow us."

The logic seemed sound enough. We proceeded down the alley and away from the two men on the street. As we proceeded, the smell of rotting garbage tickled my nose. The telltale sound of rats scurrying beneath garbage bins tickled my ears and the hair on my arms stood to attention.

Then the scurrying was accompanied by a high pitched wail somewhere nearby- maybe a couple blocks away. All of us froze dead in our tracks. I peered over my shoulder to the mouth of the alley. All of my muscles were taut and ready- I felt the way I used to as a kid before running a relay race, except this time, I was riddled with fear. I swallowed as the scream reached an even higher pitch.

Then another scream somewhere farther away was added to the mix. The two screams played off of one another like a wolf's howl.

Fynn snapped his fingers up ahead of us to get our attention. We turned back to him and followed as he started walking again. I noticed the hunch in his shoulders and the way he had drawn the collar of his shirt up higher to his jaw. The screams unsettled him just as much as they did me.

We crept back out on to another street with our backs hunched and knees bent. Keeping low, we followed the line of parked cars down the sidewalk, staying out of view of a few people in the middle of the road who were wandering aimlessly about with their mouths hanging open. I noticed that most of them had jaws that were stained in blood. At least, I assumed it was blood.

Each step brought us closer to the station with paralyzing slowness. I resisted the urge to run. I had that same feeling gnawing at my chest that I used to feel when I was a little girl fleeing from a dark room. I used to imagine that a monster was snapping at my heels as soon as the lights went out at the inky blackness engulfed me. I would run to the first source of light- usually my mother's bedroom or the living room.

I hated that feeling as it unfurled itself within me. Fear.

Kent made a hissing sound behind us. Cassidy and I turned together to look at him. He had stopped walking and was looking down a narrow alley on the opposite side of the street. In the dim light between the buildings- a cafe and a vintage clothing shop- was the figure of a woman. She was standing stone still with her head tilted so far to the right that it was almost resting on her shoulder. I was certain that she was staring right at us.

"Don't move," Kent said under his breath.

I hadn't planned to. My feet felt like they were glued to the pavement as I stared at the shadow that covered her face. I couldn't make out her features. I licked my lips uneasily. Cassidy was tense beside me. I didn't dare turn my head to look for Fynn.

At the end of the alley behind the woman another silhouette emerged. This one was faster moving, and male. He seemed to shuffle down the alley on a twisted leg. He stopped when he reached the woman. His head imitated hers and leaned to the right.

"I don't like this," Fynn hissed from a few feet ahead of us.

Had two deranged freaks not been staring at me from the depths of a creepy alley, I would have told Fynn to stuff it.

Another man appeared and joined the two who were watching us. He was followed by another, and then another, until there were nearly a dozen of them standing together like a patient pack of wolves.

"We need to move," Fynn said, and he took a step. I heard his boot crunch softly on the pavement.

Each and every one of the crazies in the alley immediately straightened their heads and fixed their attention on Fynn. He froze. A blood curdling scream bellowed out of the alley. Soon all of the people in there were screaming. Then they dropped their heads and ran straight for us.

I screamed. Kent started running and shoved me in the

back. I staggered forward and Cassidy grabbed on to my wrist. We ran like I had never run before. My thighs screamed with burning fire after we had made it half a block. I wanted to look back. I could hear the freaks behind us still screaming like banshees and I knew they were closing the distance.

The station was getting close. Fynn was running up ahead of us like a madman. His arms pumped at his sides and he was shouting for us to hurry up. The screaming behind us urged me forwards more than Fynn's cries. I didn't want to find out what would happen to me if I fell behind and the pack got their hands on me. Or *in* me.

Our feet thudded to a stop on the pavement when we reached the station doors.

"What if there's more inside?" Cassidy shrieked as Fynn grabbed the door.

"Only one way to find out," he said, yanking the door towards him and slipping inside. I didn't waste any more time. I followed him in. Cassidy and Kent were quick on our heels. "Come on!" Fynn yelled as he took off running again.

Through the glass I could see the freaks hurrying after us. One slammed head first into the glass door. The others followed suit, colliding with the glass windows and hammering their fists against it. The windows shook under the force. I took a couple hurried steps backwards before turning around and running after the others.

We rounded the corner to the station's Hall, which housed a row of ticket counters boxed in with glass frames and fixed with a speaker for the employees to speak to the customers. I skidded to a stop and slammed into Fynn's back. He steadied me by grabbing my elbow.

We were staring at a horde of mangled, bloody, disjointed people. They were staring back. There had to be at least thirty of them. Suitcases and smaller bags littered the floor. These people had been travellers. They were supposed to catch the train but never made it. Whatever this was, it had gotten to them.

Their lips all parted. Their jaws dropped open and hung

impossibly wide, exposing open throats and bloody teeth. I swallowed. They started screaming.

A door behind one of the ticket counters slammed open. A man shouted at us. He was clean- at least, there was no blood on him. He looked to be nearing sixty. He had thick gray eyebrows above his wide and terrified eyes. "This way!" He called to us.

We weren't in any position to decline his offer. We rushed forward as the horde raced to meet us head on. We made it to the door first. The man stepped aside and we all rushed through. He drew it closed behind him and locked it.

I had stumbled face first into somebody. They were big and solid and smelled like oil and exhaust. I looked up as a pair of big hands took hold of my upper arms and pushed me away. The man, well over six feet tall and dressed in blue coveralls, looked down his nose at me. His eyes flicked to the ticket counters and the crazed people wandering around outside. "You alright there, Girlie?" His whisper crackled, revealing that he was a heavy smoker. The name tag in front of my eyes read 'Bryce'.

"Y-yes," I stammered, keeping my own voice as quiet as possible, "thank you."

He dropped his arms and looked at the rest of us. "What the hell were you kids doing out there? You trying to get yourselves killed?"

"No," I answered for everyone, "we need to get to Seattle."

Bryce stared down at me again, apparently unimpressed with my answer. His mouth was set in a firm line as he rubbed his whiskery jaw with his thumb and forefinger. "The four of you," he scanned us with cold eyes, "are going to try to get into the city on your own?"

"That's the plan," I said as assertively as I could manage.

Bryce's scowl softened. He clutched his belly and threw his head back with laughter. He dabbed at the corner of his eyes with calloused and oil stained thumbs. Then he hollered over his shoulder. Another man appeared dressed in the same coveralls. His name tag read 'Kyle'. He was just as tall as Bryce, but he was all bone and no muscle. "You lot are mental," Kyle said in a voice that was lower than I had expected.

There were two women there as well. They were both well dressed in black pencil skirts and white blouses. They wore a silk royal blue scarf around their necks. Their hair was slicked back in neat buns. I realized that they must work at the station.

One of them, a read head with the greenest eyes I had ever seen, shook her head at Bryce and Kyle before turning towards us with a soft smile. "Things aren't what they were, if you haven't noticed," she said as delicately as possible, "reaching the city might be impossible. No train has come through since last night. Communications are down. Everything has just... stopped." She bit the inside of her cheek. "I'm Monica, by the way. This is Stacey." She gestured at the other woman in the pencil skirt.

Stacey nodded weakly at us but stayed where she was, standing slightly behind Monica.

"How long have you all been hiding in here?" Fynn asked.

Monica clasped her hands in front of her. "Since it all started. Since yesterday around five o'clock. The last train blew through and was carrying a bunch of these... things. They came out of the train in a frenzy and started eating people. We locked ourselves in here and have been sitting tight hoping someone might come get us out."

"There isn't anyone," Fynn stated, "the whole town has been turned into those freaks."

"They're dead," Bryce said.

We all turned to stare at him. My tongue felt like it was glued to the roof of my mouth. I forced myself to speak. "What do you mean, they're dead? They were walking around and had no problem chasing after us-"

"We saw it happen first hand, Girlie. They took down one of the boys who worked at our mechanic shop. Kyle and I saw him get eaten- at least, they ate some of him. Fifteen minutes later he stood up, his guts and shit spilling out of him. Then he just up and walked off. I'm telling you, he was dead. They all are."

"That's impossible," Cassidy whispered.

Bryce shrugged. "Maybe. But it's what's going on. If you get taken down by one of those things, it's going to tear you apart, and you're going to come back after with an appetite for human flesh. Talk about a sadistic delicacy." He smirked as if he was proud of the joke. I fought down the urge to throw up.

The old man who had brought us to safety cleared his throat. "Why do you want to get to Seattle?"

I opened my mouth to speak, but Fynn answered first. "We have people we need to find there. And, if we're lucky, the city won't be hit as bad as here. Maybe the response teams got it under control. Maybe these things don't have free reign like they do here. It's worth a shot."

The old man nodded slowly. I saw that he had a name tag as well; his name was Winston. He sighed and scratched the back of his head. "Well, no trains are coming through lad. The only way you're getting out of here is if you have someone capable of driving it."

Fynn narrowed his eyes. "We have someone capable of driving it, don't we? He just needs to offer." Winston blinked at Fynn who stared back at the older man blankly. "No point in lying, old man. I've been on your train before. You're a Conductor."

Winston chuckled. "Clever lad. If there's a train out there I can operate it- I have the keys for each girl on those tracks. But I'm in no shape to fight those things. I'm an old man and I'm not keen on becoming finger food."

"The alternative is we stay here. There's no food, no water, and no telling how long it will be until someone comes for us. *If* someone comes for us," Fynn said.

Winston was shaking his head back and forth. "I don't like it. I don't like it at all."

"None of us like it, old man," Fynn said, "but you're our only option. You have to get us out of here."

Winston caught my eye for the briefest moment. I tried to offer him a reassuring smile. "Please?" I asked. "You're not going to be out there alone. We'll all be with you. We need your help. Fynn is right- we could be locked in here for days. Maybe more.

Seattle is our best shot."

"You're asking me to put a lot of trust in a group of strangers," Winston said.

"We're all putting our trust in a group of strangers," I told him, "we're all in the same position, here. Everyone is scared. If we could do this without you, we would. But we can't. We have to get to the city. The longer we wait the more we risk. We have to go." I couldn't help but feel a surge of emotion as thoughts of my mother and sister raced through my mind.

Winston wrung his hands and his eyes darted back and forth between Fynn and I. "I suppose there's sense in that." He scratched at the whiskers under his chin. "If you keep me safe, I'll get you to Seattle."

A quietness had settled around us. The moaning and shuffling of the crazed people on the other side of the ticket counters had all but disappeared, and the sound of nothing was just as comforting as Winston's willingness to help us get to the city.

Relief flooded through me. I reached out and took one of Winston's hands in mine. "Thank you," I said earnestly.

"Alright then, it's settled," Fynn nodded. He turned to the mechanics and the two train station employees. "You lot coming?"

Stacey and Monica looked back and forth between one another. Stacey nodded finally. "We're coming."

Kyle and Bryce nodded as well. "Count us in. We have your back, old man."

I felt relief flood through me as I stared at the group of strangers. Monica and Stacey were pressed up close to one another. I noticed they were holding hands. They were just as scared as I was. Kyle had beads of sweat on his forehead and upper lip. He was pale. Bryce's fingers were twitching nervously at his sides.

We were a sorry group, but I was thankful for the numbers. I was thankful for their willingness to take a chance on us.

Winston nodded. "Alright. Follow me then. We'll go through the back here. We can cut through the break rooms.

There's an emergency door that lets out on the train platform. It's a straight shot to the train. Once we're on it'll take me a minute to close the doors. We go to the front wagon. Keep the kooks out until I get the doors closed. Alright?"

We all nodded in unison.

"Alright," Winston said more to himself than to us, "follow me then."

Winston led us out through a door with a white sign that said 'Employees Only'. We wove through a maze of hallways until we reached an emergency exit door. Bryce took the lead and shouldered the door open a crack. He peered outside as we all held our breath behind him. Finally he swung it open the rest of the way.

Bright sunlight lit up the hall and burned my eyes. I used my hand as a visor when we stepped out on to the platform. Winston pointed to the left, down the platform, to the front of the train. He started walking towards it and we all fell into step behind him.

"Keep your wits about you," Bryce muttered from somewhere behind me. "Those kooks show up out of nowhere, I tell you. Like damn feral dogs."

No one said anything to answer Bryce's warning. We continued walking, our attention fixed on the front wagon of the train. I wiped my sweaty palms on my shorts before shaking my hands out anxiously. I took a deep steadying breath- which hitched in my throat when I glanced to my left and spotted a man standing inside the station.

He was leaning slightly to his left. His head was tilted further to the side. He was too far away to make out his eyes through the glass, but I could have sworn he was staring right at me. His jeans were soaked with blood. There was a chunk missing out of his stomach.

I realized it was Harry from the hardware store. His thick beard looked darker, somehow. He pressed his forehead against the glass door and began walking. It gently swung open, allowing him to stagger through it.

He stared at us as we kept walking. His head followed our progress with a slow turn. His mouth was hanging open- much like the woman's who had taken the bite out of his belly in the bar last night. He shuffled a few feet closer. I could see his eyes now. My memory told me Harry had brown eyes; staring at him now was a contradiction to that memory. His eyes looked pale and glazed over, like he had suddenly contracted a serious case of cataracts. I couldn't stop staring at those white, milky orbs. The lack of a pupil was unsettling.

"H-hey," I stammered, trying to get the attention of the others. I was too afraid to take my eyes off Harry.

Silhouettes began to appear behind him on the other side of the glass. The station had somehow filled with people. They were pressing themselves up against the windows. Some of them, the ones who had been lucky enough to find themselves on the other side of a door, emerged on the platform behind Harry.

"Cassidy," I breathed.

She ignored me. Or she didn't hear me. It didn't matter. Harry's head turned more dramatically to the side. It was a nearly impossible angle. Those frosted eyes never left me.

Suddenly the air was ripped apart as a scream exploded out of Harry's gaping mouth. I slapped my hands over my ears and my scream echoed with Harry's as he charged forwards, head first, straight towards us.

Our only chance of escape was to make it on the train. The station doors were too far away. Harry would surely be upon us before we made it half way back. I thought, for a split second, of a squirrel running across the road and freezing in place. I always stopped for the little rodents. Harry wasn't going to stop for us. He was going to try to kill us. With his teeth.

Someone's hands yanked me sideways. I fell to my side on the pavement. My hip took most of the impact. I scrambled backwards as Harry screamed past me and tumbled down on to the train tracks below. The speed he possessed was impossible- he had covered a good thirty feet in mere seconds. He got haphazardly to his feet and turned back to us. Then he promptly began trying to climb back up on to the platform. His bloodied fingers clawed at the pavement and his fingernails peeled back as he tried to bury them in the pavement like hooks.

Fynn's boot collided with Harry's jaw. A spray of blood painted the pavement beside me. Flecks of white were scattered through the blood and I realized they were some of Harry's teeth.

Fynn grabbed me under my arms and hauled me roughly to my feet. We both turned to face the station; the doors were vomiting out more people with empty eyes and slack jaws.

"Run!" Kent roared beside me before taking hold of Cassidy and taking off at a sprint to the front of the train.

Terror unfurled itself inside me and ripped through my body like a creature hell bent on destroying me. For a moment, I realized I had stopped breathing.

I sucked in a great gasp of air that helped to clear my head. The platform was filling with people who were all staggering and running towards us. Some of them had taken to screaming the same high pitched wail that Harry had. They came barreling towards us, their arms slack and swinging at their sides.

Fynn took my hand in his. He started running, and my legs responded in kind. We barrelled down the platform, our boots slapping against the concrete. Winston was running beside Kent as fast as his old legs would take him. I was impressed that he was able to keep up. I didn't dare look back for the others: Stacey, Monica, Kyle, and Bryce. They were on their own. I had to trust that they would be able to make it in time.

"We're not going to make it," I heard Fynn breathe beside me. We were both out of breath now. He turned and looked over his shoulder. "Winston, get to the train!"

Fynn shoved me ahead. I slowed and turned back for him. He was facing the horde of slack jawed freaks. They were nearly upon us. Seconds. They would be on us in seconds. My head was spinning. My mouth tasted like salt. My fingertips were tingling.

I braced myself for impact as the distance between us and the dead shortened. Twenty feet. Ten feet. Five feet.

CHAPTER 3

Fynn met the first attack with a right hook and a knee to the gut. The man fell to his knees, looked up at Fynn, and opened his gaping mouth even wider. He grabbed hold of the waistband of Fynn's jeans and began clawing his way up the side of Fynn's body as the second white eyed psycho charged at us.

While Fynn avoided a bite to his shoulder from the second attack, I grabbed hold of the back of the man's shirt that was clinging to Fynn's side. I dragged him off with all the strength I had and pushed him over the edge of the platform. He tumbled backwards with a shriek and landed heavily on the tracks below.

I spun to help Fynn, but he already had the second attacker down. Fynn looked to the station doors. More crazies were spilling out and rushing towards us. Bryce and Kyle were ruthlessly kicking a man on the ground who was clawing at the hem of their coveralls and screaming. Cassidy was still behind Kent, who looked unscathed.

The whistle of the train blew.

"Come on!" Kent shouted, grabbing Cassidy's hand and running to the head of the platform.

I ran after them. Fynn was hot on my heels. We blew past Bryce and Kyle who were still beating the man on the ground. Fynn yelled for the two men to hurry. They didn't seem too interested in complying. I could see the fury in their eyes as they stooped over their victim.

"Faster!" Fynn yelled behind me. His hand between my

shoulder blades pushed me ahead of him and I was forced to look away from Bryce and Kyle.

The front wagon was only another fifty feet away. The doors popped open. Kent waved for us to hurry up ahead of us.

Then, behind us, there were more screams.

"Don't look," Fynn shouted over the howls, "just keep moving!"

Monica shrieked up ahead of us when she rolled an ankle. She fell to the ground with a hard smack and I ran past her before I had processed what happened. I dug my heels in to go back for her. Fynn was there to grab my upper arm and he dragged me ruthlessly ahead.

I screamed at him to let go of me. He refused. Kent hopped through the doors on the front wagon and Cassidy jumped in with him. Stacey followed him in. We were only fifteen feet away, at most.

Fynn's hand released my arm. I continued running, my legs pumping harder than they ever had before. A hot burn had started in my calves and my thighs. My lungs were raspy and every breath was sharp and dry.

I leapt through the doors and stepped aside for Fynn.

He never came.

I looked wildly back at Kent who was hanging half out the door. He was shouting Fynn's name. Cassidy had herself pressed up against the window with her knees on one of the seats. Her fist pounded the glass. She begged Fynn to hurry.

I leaned out the door in front of Kent.

Fynn was on the ground on his back. Someone was wrapped around his legs and trying to take a bite out of him. It was a woman with bright blonde hair. I could tell that she had been wearing pink lipstick.

Fynn's boot slammed into her nose. Her pink lipstick grew red and wet. He managed to wriggle himself out from under her. He stumbled to his feet and propelled himself forward. More white eyed people were chasing after him.

The chime on the train announced that the doors would be

closing.

Kent and I jumped back out of the way. A burst of air released and the doors began sliding closed. Cassidy screamed.

Then Fynn came bursting through the door. It clamped shut behind him and the freaks that had been chasing him slammed into the plastic. They proceeded to wail and press their mouths against the door. Their lips peeled back off their teeth, revealing pale gums decorated in dark purple veins.

Fynn lay on his back on the ground. He propped himself up on his elbows and gasped for breath as the train lurched forwards.

His dark hair was matted to his sweaty forehead. Perspiration had soaked through the back of his shirt and the neckline. He fell backwards and closed his eyes. "Fuck."

Cassidy sucked in a sharp breath of air. "Oh my God," she whispered, "they're eating them."

I knelt on the seats behind her and looked out the window as the train slowly began leaving the station. Bryce and Kyle were being swarmed by the people with white eyes. Their coveralls were stained in blood. Their limbs were waving all over the place as they tried desperately to escape.

A young boy in a striped shirt took a bite out of Kyle's calf. He fell to his knees. The boy proceeded to sink his teeth into the back of Kyle's thigh. Flesh came away in his mouth and he used his fingers to push the muscley mass of tissue down his throat.

I thought I might be sick.

The train passed Monica. She was on her stomach. She was screaming for us not to leave her. One of her arms was raised and her fingers were splayed wide as she reached for us. Part of her cheek was missing. At least six people had amassed around her and were burying their hands and jaws in her open back. I caught a glimpse of her spine and had a flashback of an episode of a lion documentary I had seen in high school.

Bile rose in my throat. There was no stopping it. I leaned over and expelled the contents of my stomach on the floor. I pressed a hand to my mouth and shook my head. "This isn't… this isn't right. What's happening? What's the matter with them?"

No one answered me. The cabin hummed and gently rocked from side to side as the train gained speed. By the time we gained full speed I had managed to clear my head enough to look up at the map on the panel on the ceiling.

Fynn was still lying on his back on the ground. His wrists were crossed over his eyes.

"Where's the backpack?" I asked.

Fynn got to his feet and stared at me blankly. "One of those things got a hold of it. That's why I went down. We only have the one left. We'll ration the water."

Stacey buried her face in her hands, and began to sob. I wondered how well she and Monica had known each other. I wondered if they were as close as Cassidy and I were. The thought sent a jolt of pain and panic through me.

Had I had any energy left to cry, I would have joined her.

Instead I sank down on the seat. Cassidy sat beside me. We rested our heads together and listened to the female voice through the telecom tell us that our next stop was fifteen minutes away. She wished us an enjoyable ride and thanked us for using the train. Then soft elevator music began to play, which wasn't enough to drown out Stacey's sobbing.

The door between our wagon and the conductor's caboose slid open. Winston stood there wiping his hand across his sweaty forehead. "You're the only ones who made it?"

Kent nodded. "Yeah. The others... they're back on the platform."

Winston pinched the bridge of his nose and closed his eyes. "Alright then. Sit tight, boys and girls. It's a two hour and twenty minute straight shot to Seattle. We're safe on the tracks. I suggest you get some rest. I'll let you know when we're close."

CHAPTER 4

The train lulled me into a restless but much needed hour of sleep as it swayed gently as it barrelled down the tracks to Seattle. I had claimed one of the bench seats and used the plaid shirt tied around my waist as a pillow. Cassidy slept on the bench across from me with her knees drawn up to her chest and her cheek resting on her palm. The others were scattered in different places in the wagon. Stacey was staring out the window with her forehead pressed against the glass as green pastures flew by outside. She had cried for the first hour of our journey. Eventually she fell quiet. I suspected she was too tired to cry anymore, but too distraught to sleep.

Kent was at the back of our wagon. He was sitting up with his head resting on the back wall. His eyes were closed and his mouth was hanging open as he slept. I envied him; being able to sleep so soundly after such chaos was a luxury. I suspected I would not enjoy the pleasure of a restful sleep for a while. Or ever. The white eyes and snapping jaws of the cannibals back on the platform haunted me every second my eyes closed. I watched with jealousy as Kent's head lolled around on his shoulders as the train continued to waver from side to side.

Fynn was lying on the ground between the rows of bench seats. He was on his back with his hands crossed behind his head. One knee was bent and the other leg rested across it. His eyes were closed but I had a feeling that he wasn't sleeping. The permanent scowl he always wore was still lingering in the creases on his forehead and in the corners of his mouth. His mind was working behind those closed eyes, I was sure of it. Perhaps he was plagued with thoughts of the monsters that had tried to eat him- and nearly succeeded. He had been closer than any of us to ending up like Bryce and the others.

Someone touched my knee lightly and I jumped. My eyes flew up to Cassidy, who had sat upright and reached out to get my attention. "Sorry," she mumbled, her voice thick. She rubbed her eyes with the heels of her hands, yawned, and stretched her hands above her head. Her eyes did a quick scan of everyone else still sleeping. Her gaze lingered a little longer on Fynn, who was still scowling with his eyes closed. "Were you able to sleep at all?" She asked me, her eyes leaving Fynn and settling on me.

"Yeah, a little."

Our one remaining backpack from my house was on the floor between us. She bent over and withdrew a water bottle. She unscrewed the cap, took a small mouthful, and handed it to me. As I took a sip she rubbed her arms nervously. "Do you know if we're getting close?"

I looked out the window. Farmlands were rolling by outside. The sun was still low in the sky, casting a pink amber glow over everything. The serene beauty of it all was a stark contrast to the horror we had just escaped back at the train station. The stillness of everything outside the window made it seem as if nothing bad had actually happened; as if all was still as it should be. "I don't think it's been all that long. Maybe an hour?"

"I was hoping I'd sleep through the whole trip. I guess some of us just aren't that lucky," she cast jealous glances at the others who were still sleeping. She noticed Stacey staring out the window and her cheeks flushed. "That was cruel. She just lost her friend."

I chewed on the inside of my cheek and refused to look at Stacey. I could see the reflection of her glassy eyes in the window of the train. There was too much despair there for me to handle. The worry in my gut for my mother and sister and the anxiety of how I was going to get to them was enough for me to contend with at the moment. "Thanks for coming with me, Cassidy."

"Where else would I have gone?"

That was a fair question. Cassidy didn't have any family to speak of- not anymore. She had lost her parents when we were just out of high school in a car accident. She had lived with me and my mother and sister until she was stable enough to get her own place. It had been a rough few years, and I knew she had come out of it a stronger person than she ever got credit for.

"Not to mention," Cassidy said, "they're practically my family too. I don't know where I'd be if not for your mom. Do you have a plan for when we get to the city? Do you know where your mom might be?"

"I have a couple ideas," I said. "If she's not at the apartment she might be at the hospital. If she had an evening shift she would have brought Addison to the daycare down the block."

"So, check the daycare if they aren't at the apartment?"

"Yeah."

"Alright. You know how to get to it?"

"I remember how. I'm pretty sure, at least."

"Pretty sure?" Fynn asked from the floor to my right. I looked over at him. He was still lying on his back, but his eyes were open and he was staring at me out of the corner of his eye. "You're only pretty sure you know how to find it? I don't want to waste any time wandering around unfamiliar city streets in this mess."

"Then you shouldn't have tagged along," I said evenly.

Fynn uncrossed his leg from across his knee and sat up. "Maybe that was information you could have been more forthcoming with before we set out on this rescue mission."

"Her sister is eleven," Cassidy spoke up in my defense, "don't be such an ass. If you stayed behind you would have just holed up somewhere dark and quiet and drank yourself stupid."

"Better than almost getting eaten," Fynn said coldly.

I noticed that both of his elbows were raw and bloody. The knees of his jeans had been torn up and there was a little bit of blood there, too. When he had been taken down on the platform by the flesh-hungry goon squad he must have fallen harder than I thought. A pang of guilt came to life inside me. It could have easily been me who had been caught by those freaks. Fynn had made sure I was ahead of him the whole time.

"I should have said something earlier," I admitted, "I didn't think of it with all this going on."

Fynn made an unimpressed sound in the back of his throat.

"Thanks for helping me back there," I said, waiting for him to meet my eyes. He never did. He occupied himself with staring everywhere but at me: out the windows, at Stacey, at his own shoes- anywhere. "I don't know what would have happened if you weren't there. I owe you."

"No you don't," he said, getting to his feet and stretching. He arched his spine like a cat. I heard it crack several times as he clasped his hands above his head and reached up high. His shirt inched up and I got a second look at his flat stomach, hip bones, and dark trail of hair below his belly button. He looked over at me and he held out his hand expectantly. "You done with that?"

I blinked.

"The water," he clarified.

I felt my cheeks start to burn as I hastily handed him the bottle of water that had been sitting in my lap. He unscrewed the cap and tilted his head back. I watched his Adam's apple bob as he swallowed. There was stubble starting to appear along his jaw. A trickle of water escaped the corner of his mouth and rolled down his chin. He wiped it away with the back of his hand as he handed me the water bottle back. His eyes scrutinized my bright cheeks, and I was thankful that he didn't take the opportunity to be an ass and tease me.

In order to distract myself from the stirring in my belly from staring at Fynn, I bent down and returned the water to the backpack. I met Cassidy's eyes. She was doing her best not to laugh at me. I was horrified to realize that I was doing that poor of a job of hiding the undeniable fact that Fynn was, to my horror, insanely attractive. I was overcome with the urge to slap myself across the face to punish such petty worries at a time of crisis.

I needed to get away from Fynn and his intoxicating eyes and scowl. I grabbed the water bottle again and stood up. I brushed by him without saying anything. He watched me go as I took up a seat across from Stacey. She didn't so much as look at me.

I cleared my throat and held out the bottle of water. Her eyes left the window and she stared at me. It seemed, for a moment, that I was staring into eyes that couldn't actually see me. "You should drink," I said.

She blinked slowly and looked down at the bottle I was holding out to her. I tried to encourage her by taking the cap off. She surprised me by taking it and drinking a couple mouthfuls. She handed it back to me. "Thank you."

"Of course, we have to watch out for each other now."

She pursed her lips. There were still traces of faded red lipstick along her cupid's bow and at the corners of her mouth. She looked like the sort of woman who would check her reflection once every hour or so an apply more lip color as needed. "Yeah, I guess," Stacey said softly.

"If you don't want to talk about it you don't have to... but, did you know her well? Monica? I'm sorry for what happened. She seemed like a good person."

Stacey surprised me by laughing. It was a bitter sound that drew the attention of Fynn and Cassidy on the other side of the aisle. "She wasn't."

"Oh," I said lamely.

"She didn't deserve what happened to her though," Stacey said firmly, "no one deserves that."

"You're right."

I sat with Stacey for a little while longer. We didn't say anything. The silence was uncomfortable but not unbearable. She resumed staring out the window and I sat restlessly thinking about my mom and Addison. I had terrible thoughts of what the city might be like. I had to suppress signs of panic attacks as soon as they hit: burning chest, racing thoughts, quickened breath. If I thought too long about my family I would lose control. My palms would get sweaty. An ache would begin in my ribs. I couldn't afford to give in to the panic right now. There was too much at stake.

In order to distract myself, I tried to get Stacey talking again. "So, what exactly happened back at the station?"

"Does it matter?"

I bit my bottom lip. "It matters to me. I'm still trying to figure out what this whole thing is. At some point it has to all make sense, right?"

"It has to make sense?" Stacey asked. "You want to apply sense to this? Monica and those mechanics were *eaten alive.* There is no sense in that."

"I could have phrased it better. I meant that there has to be an explanation. People don't just start eating other people. Especially not with that much... vigor."

Stacey laughed incredulously and leaned towards me. Her eyes were wide and wild as she fixed me with a stare that looked entirely out of place on her slender face. For a moment I could barely recognize her. Images of the white eyes of the freaks at the station flashed behind my eyelids when I blinked. As I stared back at Stacey, I couldn't help but feel the same emptiness in her eyes that I had felt the first time I saw one of the monsters. I shook my head to clear the vision, and as I did so, Stacey jabbed her finger at me accusingly. Her lips curled back off her teeth as she said, "you have some nerve, you obnoxious self serving-"

Fynn arrived at the end of my bench seat. He lifted a leg and rested his knee on the edge of Stacey's seat. I dimly wondered if he would leave some blood stains behind. Then I realized it didn't matter. People were eating each other. We had bigger problems than trying to wash blood out of red cloth seats. I turned my attention back to Stacey. She was slowly leaning backwards and glaring up at Fynn. He was staring back with just as much intensity. She was irritated and flustered by the interruption. Had he not arrived I was sure she would have gone off the deep end. She already seemed to have cracked. The wild look in her eyes was still there like a ghost lying in wait.

"There's no need to get nasty," Fynn said quietly, looking calmly back and forth between Stacey and I. "Although it may seem like an insensitive question, I think Violet has a good reason for asking it. So I'll ask again on her behalf. What happened back at the station?"

Stacey narrowed her eyes at him. She crossed her arms across her chest and her cleavage winked at me between the collar of her button up blouse. "There's not much to tell."

Fynn sat down beside me and leaned forward, resting his elbows on his knees. He pressed the tips of his fingers together and looked up at Stacey from beneath his dark brows. She returned his stare with all the bravado she was able to muster. He wasn't backing down. "Any information could be helpful."

Kent had stirred awake at the back of the wagon. He was getting to his feet and making his way over as Stacey continued to glower at Fynn and I. Kent took a seat across from Cassidy. They both turned to face us so that we made an intimidating group of five. All of us stared at Stacey expectantly.

"Fine," she said through clenched teeth. She crossed her legs. She looked like a folded up pretzel with her arms and legs all wrapped around each other. "My shift had just started. I clocked in and was in the middle of putting my uniform on when Monica came running into the back room. She closed and locked the door behind her. She was terrified. I asked her a hundred times what was wrong, and she just kept telling me to be quiet. So I listened to her. I did what she said. Even when people were screaming on the other side of the door and pounding their fists on it, begging for us to let them in, I listened to her. We stayed in there, just the two of us, while everyone else outside was... was..." She looked away from us and swallowed a couple times.

"You can skip some of it," I offered, "if it's too hard to say."

Stacey didn't acknowledge that I had said anything. "We must have stayed in there for at least three hours. It had been quiet for a while- dead quiet- when we finally worked up the nerve to go outside. We left the break room. No one was out in the halls. They must have all ran out on to the platform. I don't know. We came out into the ticket hall and found Winston, Kyle and Bryce. They had locked themselves behind the glass wickets. Some of the glass was smeared with blood. Winston told me not to look. He told me I didn't need to see.'

"But I needed to," Stacey continued. "I needed to know what was out there. So I looked. The hall was a mess. The floors were dark with blood and there were bodies everywhere. Half eaten, mangled, fucked up bodies. I asked how it happened. Bryce told me that people just started eating each other. I didn't believe him. Of course I didn't believe him." She wiped at her eyes as tears began to fall. "Then, on the platform, when they... when those things got a hold of them... I knew it was true. This is it. This is what it's all come to."

I looked over at Fynn. He glanced at me. I turned back to Stacey. "What do you mean, this is what it's come to?"

She laughed. The sound was bitter and held no humor in it. She leaned back against the seat and shook her head. "It's not rocket science. This is how it ends for us. This is our destruction. You think we're just going to arrive in city central and be able to find your baby sister and dear sweet mom? You're naive. You all are. Everyone is dead. And if they aren't yet, it's just a matter of time. You can all feel it in your bones, just like me."

Every cell in my body was screaming at me to hit her; to pound her teeth in with my knuckles and crack her ribs with my knees and elbows. Instead I took a deep breath and blew out through my nose. "*If* my family is dead, maybe I'll be just as angry and empty as you are."

"Maybe," Stacey said venomously, "now leave me alone. All of you. You got your story. Go have your little pow wow somewhere else."

I stood up. I had no interested in sitting with her any longer. I stepped around Fynn who has doing a poor job of hiding how irritated he was. He stood behind me and followed me to the back of the train. Cassidy and Kent were hot on his heels. We all settled down on the benches at the back. Fynn took the spot beside me and Cassidy sat across from me. Kent opted to stand with his back resting against the window. He cast a troubled look down the aisle to Stacey's back. "She going to be this much fun to be around the whole time?"

"Who cares?" I said. "If she wants to be mad at us, let her."

Kent shrugged. "Alright. Fine. I wasn't the one who looked like I was going to explode and beat the shit out of her."

I blushed fiercely again.

"I was almost hoping it would happen," Kent continued, "I mean, it would have been a show. Your fists were clenched and your knuckles went pure white. I thought I was going to have to get a snack while the show went on."

"Shut up," Cassidy said, rolling her eyes, "it wouldn't have been a show. I've seen Vi when she's pissed. It would have been over as soon as it started, let me tell you."

Cassidy's words didn't help the burning in my cheeks. "Stop it."

She shrugged. "It's true. You're a badass. I've seen it in action."

"Thanks for the vote of confidence."

Cassidy grinned. "You're welcome."

Kent clapped his hands and rubbed them together. "Alright, when are we going to talk seriously about what happened back there?"

"If you have something to say, just say it," Fynn said.

"Suits me." Kent dropped down on the seat so close to Cassidy that he was nearly sitting in her lap. She inched away from him but he didn't seem to notice. "We saw what happened to those mechanics and Stacey's friend. Those freaks almost got you too, Fynn. We need to prepare ourselves. We might be facing more of those in the city."

"Or none," I added.

"Or none," Kent said, his voice sounding thin and unconvinced, "but I think it's safer to assume that the city will be knee deep in this shit too. We need weapons. We need to be able to defend ourselves."

"I packed knives," Fynn said casually. "Front zipper of the

backpack. They're wrapped in a kitchen towel."

"You stole my kitchen knives?" I asked.

"Borrowed," Fynn corrected, lifting one finger in the air matter of factly.

"Good," Kent said, "we'll probably need them."

"Um," Cassidy said nervously, "I don't want to go sticking Vi's steak knives into people. Sorry, not down for that."

"You'd rather they eat you?" Kent asked.

"No, of course not, but-"

"There's not but," Kent said, "those freaks will try to eat you. You saw what they did. They went full on psycho trying to get to us. We need a way to protect ourselves if we get into a tight spot."

"I agree," I said.

Cassidy stared at me with wide eyes. "What? You're seriously considering this? We're talking about killing people, Violet. Killing people with carving knives you bought second hand at a thrift store. What the fuck?"

I looked at Fynn and Kent. They knew what had to be done. They didn't need any convincing, and neither did I. My mom and Addison were counting on me. "I don't think they're people anymore, Cassidy."

"Of course they're people, Vi, what do you mean-"

"Back on the platform, before they charged us, one of them was staring at me. His eyes were all glazed over. I've seen that before. He was dead. I'm sure of it. They all are. They have wounds that people can't survive. Some of them were half eaten. They were missing limbs and belly's and throats. You don't keep walking after that, let alone running full speed and still possessing the strength to bring down two strong men like Bryce and Kyle."

"What are you saying?" Cassidy asked.

"I'm saying that you shouldn't feel bad if you have to kill one of them, because they're already dead."

My words hung between us like a thick and heavy fog. Nobody spoke. Everyone sat in silence with their own thoughts raging in their head. I knew I had dropped a bomb. I knew it was a stretch, but I also knew that my three companions weren't stupid. They would see reason. They would see the truth in what I was saying, and if that saved Cassidy and gave her the courage to protect herself, it was worth it.

"She's right," Fynn said finally, "they're not who they were anymore. When I went down on the platform I was up close and personal with one of those things. It wasn't a person anymore. It wasn't right- wasn't normal."

"Irregular," Kent said.

"Yeah, very," Fynn said.

"That's what we should call them," Kent said, "Irregulars. Better than crazies or freaks or kooks."

"Irregulars," I said, the word filling my mouth with distaste. I nodded. "It works."

"So, let me just get this straight," Cassidy said, "when the train stops in Seattle we're going to get off and head into the city armed with Vi's kitchen knives in case we have to fight any zombies?"

All three of us nodded at her.

Cassidy pressed a hand to her forehead. "Jesus Christ. We're all going to die."

"No," I said hurriedly, "we're not. Not if we stick together. We don't know what the city will be like. It has to be better than Lynden. The police won't have let this get out of control. It will be contained. It has to be. We can get to my mom and sister. They'll know where to go after that. There'll be somewhere people can go to be safe."

"Maybe," Cassidy said.

"Do you have any better ideas?" I asked, unable to hide the irritation that colored my voice. "If you do, I'm all ears."

Cassidy looked at the floor. She sighed and shook her head. "No, you know I don't."

"Okay, then we're all on the same page. Right?"

The three of them nodded at me. I saw, for the shortest moment, a smile on Fynn's lips as he stared at me. He stood and slapped his hands on his thighs. The smile vanished and was replaced with his brooding scowl. "Sit tight," he said before leaving and heading back to the benches Cassidy and I had originally been sitting in. He returned with a bundle tucked under his arm. I recognized my red and blue floral dish towel instantly. He put it down on the empty seat beside me and unwrapped it, revealing half a dozen blue handled knives.

Kent raised an eyebrow and looked at me. "You couldn't have been the kind of girl who buys quality, hey?"

I blushed yet again and looked back down at the knives. "I bought them for chopping tomatoes and broccoli, not for killing people."

"Irregulars," Kent corrected. He plucked one of the knives from the towel and tucked it into his belt. Fynn did the same. Cassidy and I followed suit. I was acutely aware of the sharp point of the knife by my hip. I wished I had something to cover it so I didn't stab myself with it.

"What about the other two?" Cassidy asked.

"One for the old man," Fynn said, "and one for the ticket chick."

"Stacey," I said.

"Whatever," Fynn said, waving his hand. "She can have hers when we get off the train. I don't see a need to hand her a weapon right now. She might try to cut your pretty eyeballs out, Violet," he winked at me.

I rolled my eyes. Fynn chuckled.

The door at the front of the wagon burst open. Winston stood there, his chest rising and falling with labored breaths as he looked wildly about. His gaze landed on us at the back of the wagon. He hobbled down the aisle, nodding at Stacey as he passed her. He drew to a stop when he was beside us and took a moment to collect his breath.

"What's wrong?" I asked, my heart fluttering wildly in my chest.

"Distress call," he said breathlessly, "just came in. There are people stranded at one of the stops outside the city. Six of them. Two are children. They're broadcasting their call and my communications system picked up on it."

"Broadcast system?" Fynn asked. "You didn't think to mention you had a way of contacting people earlier?"

Winston shook his head. "I can only contact other stations and trains. It's a private line. I can't radio back to them, I can only hear their distress call."

"What did they say?" Kent asked.

"That there are six of them locked in the control room. They have no water. Two of them are already dead. They need help."

"What are you proposing, old man?" Fynn asked in a monotonous tone.

Winston turned to me before he spoke. His wrinkly old eyes were worried. "I'm proposing that we might want to consider helping them. We might be their only shot."

"Are you mad?" Stacey had emerged over Winston's shoulder. There were dark stains on her cheeks from her mascara. She had been crying again. Now she looked furious. "You want us to stop and help a bunch of strangers after what happened to us? We lost three people. We have no idea what we'd be getting ourselves into."

"I hate to agree with her," Fynn said coldly, "but she has a point. Sounds more like a suicide mission than a rescue."

"We barely got out alive back there," Cassidy said nervously.

I looked at Kent. He stared back at me wordlessly. I bit my bottom lip. "So we drive right by them and don't give it a second thought? We leave them to starve, or be eaten?"

"Someone might come for them," Cassidy said pleadingly.

"Or, more than likely, someone won't," I retorted. "We could use more people. Strength in numbers."

"He said two of them were children," Stacey said. "Not exactly the right candidates for a mini army to go into the city and fetch your family. Besides, what makes you think they'd even want to help us?"

"I'd ask them to. They don't have to. You don't either. We

can go our separate ways when we get to Seattle. In fact, I'd love if we went our separate ways. Do I need to remind you that your ass would still be locked in behind that ticket counter if we hadn't come along?"

Stacey crossed her arms again and glared at me. "Yeah, and maybe Monica and the others would still be alive."

"Not for long," I retorted, "don't kid yourself. You all needed to get out of there."

"We should stop," Kent said suddenly. "They have kids with them. We can't just leave them to their fate and hope they figure it out."

"We could die before we even get to them," Cassidy said.

"We could die as soon as we set foot in Seattle," Kent said, "everything is risky now. But we should still do what's right... shouldn't we?"

"Yes," I said.

"No," Fynn said seconds after, "we should do what keeps us alive. I don't want to try my luck again out there unless I have to. And this is a choice. We don't *have* to stop. We can keep going. We can get straight to your family, Violet. Isn't that what you want?"

"Of course it is, but-"

"Then you need to put them first," he said decisively, "you can't play the hero every time someone needs a helping hand."

"I'm not playing the hero," I hissed, "but I don't know how I could knowingly just drive by people who are going to die when I had the chance to do something about it."

"So, in other words, playing the hero," Fynn stated.

"You can call it whatever you want," I said, "I don't care."

"It's three against three," Kent said, "what are we going to do about that?"

I looked imploringly at Cassidy. I was hoping she would cave and come to her senses. She wasn't the sort to ever abandon those in need. She had been my protector in high school when the bullies sought me out and tried to make my life a living hell. Cassidy had stood firm and taught me how to stare them down and hold my ground. She was the reason I had been able to tell Stacey off without flinching. Sixteen years old me would have tucked my tail between my legs and submitted at the first sign on conflict.

"Cassidy," I pleaded, "please?"

She was looking at Fynn. She hung her head. "I just don't think it's smart, Violet. I'm sorry."

I groaned in frustration and buried my face in my hands. I rubbed my eyes so forcefully that some of my eyelashes came away on my fingertips. I looked up at the ceiling, took a deep breath, and closed my eyes. "Alright," I said, "alright. Can we stop at that station, Winston? Get a look at things? If it's overrun, we keep going. If it's deserted, and it looks like we can get in and out without a fight, we help those people. Can we all agree on that, at least?"

"Sounds fair," Kent said, looking at the others hopefully.

Stacey surprised me by shrugging her shoulders. "Fine."

Fynn was watching me evenly. "We stop for a look. If it's a lost cause you'll be able to keep going?"

"I won't have a choice," I said.

Fynn nodded and looked at Winston. "You can stop on the platform but keep the doors closed?"

"Not a problem," Winston assured him.

"Okay," Fynn said, "can you get on board with this, Cassidy?"

Cassidy nodded slowly and absently ran her finger over the handle of the knife on her belt. "Yeah. Yeah, I can."

"Thank you," I breathed, not realizing how tense I had been. I ran my palms over my thighs and rolled my shoulders.

Winston headed back up the aisle to the front of the train. He looked over his shoulder at us. "Better get yourselves ready, there's only ten minutes of track between us and the station."

CHAPTER 5

The track ran straight for a good two miles, giving us the opportunity to press our faces against the windows as the station came into view. It was bigger than the one we had in Lynden, and much more modern. It was two stories high and as we drew to only a quarter mile away, I could see sunlight reflecting off glass windows that made up the entire back of the building. I realized that the station was attached to a much larger building on the right hands side. The exterior was red brick and there were very few windows. I suspected it could be a shopping mall or warehouses.

I could also see the shapes of dozens of people staggering around the platform. I didn't want to be the one to point this out to the others. It didn't take long for Cassidy to groan loudly and pound her fist gently on the glass.

"The place is covered with them," she said, "there's no way we could get across the platform. We should tell Winston to keep going."

"No," I said quickly, "we'll stop and look. Just in case."

Cassidy bit her bottom lip as she stared at me. "Vi... what does this mean?"

Her question confused me at first. How was I supposed to answer something so vague? I narrowed my eyes at her and shrugged. "What does this mean for what?"

"For us. For Seattle. We're eighty miles from home. If these things are here don't you think they'll be in Seattle, too?"

My fingertips started to tingle and I felt momentarily light headed. "I don't know."

"I know you're scared for Addison and your mom... but we need to be careful. There's more people in the city. More people to turn into these things. Maybe we're going in the wrong direction."

The worry in my gut hardened into anger. "I'm not leaving them behind."

"I never said we had to," Cassidy said hurriedly, sensing the anger brewing in me, "I just meant we need to consider the possibility that Seattle isn't as safe as we were hoping. It might be more dangerous."

I turned my attention back to the deranged walking corpses that were growing closer with every passing second. "It might be."

The train came to a stop and the wheels squealed on the tracks. Winston emerged back in our wagon and looked around at us. He turned to look out the window at the station. He wrung his hands together and his whiskery mouth hardened into a firm line. "I don't like this," he muttered, refusing to look any of us in the eye.

Fynn snapped his fingers to get our attention.

We all looked back at him. He was on his knees between two of the benches. He gestured for us to do the same. We followed suit, sliding into other spaces. I ended up beside Fynn and was acutely aware of the warmth of his hip pressed against mine.

Kent and Cassidy crouched down in the aisle in front of us, while Winston and Stacey ducked into the one ahead of them. I could hear them all whispering anxiously to one another as they peered out at the platform.

"You still want to go in there?" Fynn asked me, his voice barely a whisper.

No, I wasn't sure. I definitely wasn't sure. But the only thing I could think about were the kids inside. Maybe they were the same age as my sister. I believed in good karma. Leaving a couple kids to die of starvation in a train station control room was a decision I knew would haunt me for the rest of my life- which, now that I considered it, was potentially going to be far shorter than I had expected.

I tightened my sweater around my waist and listened to the irregulars on the platform as they sidled up to the train. I took my hair down and pulled it back up into a higher and tighter ponytail. "I don't think we have anything to lose by waiting for a bit. Twenty minutes. See if we have an opportunity to get through these things."

"Twenty minutes?" Fynn asked lazily.

"Yes, if it's still impossible to get there… then we move on to Seattle." It was a small sacrifice that could make a huge difference.

Fynn rested his head against the wall. He closed his eyes. "Twenty minutes. What could go wrong in twenty minutes?"

"That's a terrible question to ask," I said, unable to stop the smirk that curled my lips.

Fynn opened his left eye to peer over at me but didn't say anything.

I was unsure of how much time had passed when Fynn inched away from the wall and rested on the balls of his feet. He crouched below the window and inched himself upwards so that his eyes were just above the window ledge.

"What do you see?" I whispered.

He held his finger vertically across his lips. He was watching the window with intense curiosity. He motioned me forward with one hand. I crept up beside him and rested my fingers against the window sill. I peered out across the platform to a swarm of irregulars who were lazily roaming about, their arms hanging at their sides and their blank eyes scanning the length of our train. They seemed less than enthused by our arrival, and soon most of them lost interest in the train. One, however, stood out to me; an exceptionally tall man with blood matted brown hair and solid white eyes that looked like glowing orbs. His head twitched from left to right and his eyes remained unfocused. He was blind.

I pressed my index finger against the glass to point at the

tall irregular. "That one," I whispered, "I think it's blind."

Fynn nodded as he followed the direction I was pointing in. "He's listening," Fynn said.

"For what?"

"Why don't you ask him?" Fynn said irritably.

I fell silent and looked back out at the tall irregular. He was in front of the glass station doors. His head was turned dramatically to the right so I could see the side of his face. Part of his cheek was missing. If we had been closer I would have been able to see his teeth. He was motionless except for his fingers, which were twitching chaotically at his sides. His head jerked and he staggered to his right, where he promptly pressed his ear to the glass.

"Do you think he can hear the people inside?" I whispered as quietly as I could manage.

"I don't know," Fynn said, "he's definitely listening for something."

I spotted another one of the irregulars standing motionless by one of the covered benches on the platform. It was a woman. She was wearing one shoe- a sleek, patent leather pump- and a black pantsuit. A business woman. Her hair was drawn back in a sleek bun and her face was angled up at the sky. Her fingers twitched manically, just like the taller male irregular. I pointed her out to Fynn. "Another one."

"Yeah," he breathed, "I see her."

It became quickly apparent that several of the irregulars were blind. I spotted two more of them. They all exhibited the same characteristics: blankly staring at nothing while their fingers twitched, with their heads always angled to the side, and their mouths slightly open.

"Do you think they all go blind, eventually?" I asked.

Fynn shrugged one shoulder. "No idea."

Discussing this sort of thing wasn't going to get us anywhere. Fynn had just as much information as I did at this point- which was basically nothing. I shifted my weight to my other leg as my knees started to cramp up. "Do you see a way in?" I asked.

I thought Fynn would have scolded me for still wanting

to get into the station. Instead his eyes scanned the building and he crept a little higher to get a better look at the platform. He pointed to the right- at the building attached to the station. "It's deserted down there. One of those back doors might be unlocked. If not, we can try to make our way around the side and go in through the front. We'd be moving blind, though. We don't know what it's like on the other side."

I squinted to see the doors he was talking about. They were painted the same color as the brick walls and I hadn't noticed them at first. It was definitely a mall. Those doors would open into a hallway for staff and store owners only. "I doubt one will be open."

"Got a better idea?" He asked with a scowl. "If people were running out of there in a hurry to escape being eaten alive, chances are they left some of the doors unlocked. It's the best move we can make."

Kent appeared behind us. He had crawled over on his hands and knees from where he had been hiding two aisles down. "Are we still going to do this?"

I looked between him and Fynn. My stomach was swirling with nerves. I could hear my own blood rushing in my ears. Words were, for the moment, impossible. My tongue was glued to the roof of my mouth and felt like and useless.

"Yeah," Fynn said, "but we have to move quietly. That tall one out there is listening. If he hears us, we're done for. We climb out the train windows," he nodded his chin at the windows on the other side of the wagon, "and go around the train. We can use it for cover. When the coast is clear we get to the closest service door. We try them all until we get in. Then we regroup and go from there."

"We don't have time to waste trying to find this control room," Kent muttered.

"I agree," I said, managing to make my mouth work again. "We don't know what's in there. There could be hundreds of them. Do we want to risk our lives doing this-"

"This was your idea," Fynn hissed, "and now you have cold

feet?"

"Can you blame me?" I asked, my temper flaring. "If we have no idea where the control room is we could get ourselves killed in there trying to find it. I want to help these people, but I don't want to die trying. I don't want any of us to die trying."

"Hold up a minute," Kent said before shimmying back across the floor to the other aisle of seats. Fynn and I waited in silence for his return. He was back within thirty seconds. "Winston thinks this station is similar to the layout back in Lynden. Second floor, back room." Kent rose up into a crouch to look out the window. "He says the control room has a good view of the platform and the tracks. So it's probably second level, right up there," I followed the line of his pointing finger to the second story above the entrance below.

"Okay," I said.

"Then we know where we're going," Fynn said confidently, "that's better than nothing. Violet, are you in or are you out?"

"That's it?" Cassidy hissed from somewhere above my head. I looked up to find her looking down at me from the other side of the bench seat. Her fingers were wrapped so tightly around the top of the seat that her knuckles were turning white. "That's your big plan? Sneak over and try to open a door? You're going to get yourselves killed!"

"We'll be careful," I promised, "my mom and sister need me too. I'm not going to abandon them. And I won't abandon you either. Just wait here for us. We won't be long."

"So you're going, then?" She asked.

I nodded.

Cassidy's eyes were brimming with tears. "You don't have to do this." She wasn't looking at me anymore. Her wet eyes were focused on Fynn, who had fallen perfectly still beside me, like a petrified statue.

"I know," I said, unable to think of anything else to say. Fynn wasn't about to start talking to try to ease her worries. "Focus on getting ready to help us get back on the train. There will be more of us. Winston might have to open the doors if we're in a pinch."

"Okay," Cassidy nodded, her bottom lip trembling.

"I'll see you soon, Cassidy, I promise."

Cassidy nodded again and a tear escaped. She brushed it away, her cheeks flushing pink as Fynn and Kent tried to look busy staring at the roof. A crying girl was still as uncomfortable as it always had been, apparently, regardless of the zombies.

I got quietly to my feet. Fynn and Kent followed suit and made their way over to the windows on the opposite side of the train. Cassidy stood and came to stand slightly behind me. She sniffled none too quietly as Fynn unlatched the locks on the window and shimmied it open. We would be jumping down on to grass- a nice quiet landing. There was a strip of long grass, maybe knee height, that ran along the edge of the tracks. The strip was only about ten feet wide, and it abruptly ended and was met with a line of dense trees. At first I suspected a small park, but as I looked left and right, I couldn't see the end of branches and leaves. A decent sized forest.

Winston stepped up behind me and tapped me and gently took my elbow. He peered up at me from beneath his bushy gray eyebrows. "You kids be careful when you get in there, alright? You have no idea what could be in there."

"We'll be careful," I said.

"I'll be ready to go as soon as we see you coming," he said, "I'll open the doors for you if... if you're being chased."

I tried to extinguish the swirl of butterflies that took flight in my belly. The smile I gave the old train conductor was thin and I was sure he saw right through it. He rested a hand on my shoulder and gave it a soft squeeze.

I spotted Stacey standing in the corner over Winston's shoulder. Her arms were crossed and she was glowering at me with a ferocity that startled me. The hatred she seemed to feel towards me was more intense than she had a right to feel. I couldn't help but become paralyzed in her hollow stare. Her eyes were cold and detached. It unsettled me. When I turned away I could still feel her eyes on my back.

I stepped up on the seat below one of the windows. Kent climbed up on the other. Fynn remained between us and nodded for us to go ahead.

Kent went first. He lifted himself up with his hands on the frame. He managed to twist himself around so that his feet were outside the train, and he dropped down unceremoniously on to the grass seven or so feet below. Fynn went to get on the bench, but as he lifted his right leg Cassidy lurched forward and grabbed hold of his sleeve. He turned back to her, his eyes wide and confused, as she looked at her feet and blushed.

"Please be careful," she said quietly.

"I will," Fynn said uncomfortably.

Cassidy lifted her eyes to meet his blank stare. She dabbed at the tears that were appearing at the corners of her eyes. Then she glanced up at me, and, as if she were ashamed, she let go of Fynn's sleeve and took a step back. She clasped her hands in front of herself and nodded nervously at me. "You too. Look out for each other."

Fynn succeeded at getting on the bench on his second attempt. He didn't look back at Cassidy as he climbed out the window, but I was sure he must have been aware of her eyes on him as he fell to the grass on the other side.

I didn't say anything to her as I followed the boys out the window. When I got back I would ask her what that whole thing was all about. Now was not the time to let her emotions get the best of her. Not only that, but I was fairly certain that Fynn wasn't the sort of guy to cater to a girl who had a crush on him when the world around us was literally falling apart- unless she showered him with bottles of liquor.

When I landed on the grass we all remained perfectly still and waited for the telltale sounds of the moaning and groaning of the irregulars. It never came. We hadn't been heard. We snuck our way up to the front of the train and padded quietly out on to the tracks. I peeked around the corner of the train. None of the irregulars were looking in our direction. Most were fixated on trying to get back into the building.

I ignored the feeling of panic in my chest and stepped up on to the platform. Kent and Fynn did the same, and we jogged on the balls of our feet to the back wall of the mall, where we stopped at the first service door. I gritted my teeth against the anxiety as I prayed the door was unlocked.

It wasn't.

I stared down the wall at the glass portion of the station. We hadn't been spotted. We hurried down to the next door. Locked. I resisted the urge to curse. Uttering a single word could be a death sentence out here. The third door was also locked.

The fourth swung open when Kent twisted the handle desperately. He lunged inside and caught hold of it before it banged against the wall on the other side. Then we stepped in and closed the door silently behind us.

We were instantaneously plunged into an inky darkness that made it nearly impossible to see more than ten feet ahead of us. I looked to our right and saw the weakest glowing red light. I nudged Fynn in the ribs with my elbow. He mumbled under his breath and I grabbed hold of him and turned him to face the light. "There," I said, "exit. Let's go."

"Move quietly," Fynn reminded us as we made our way down the narrow hallway.

It was hard to be as quiet as he wanted us to be. My shoes tapped the concrete below and I had to slow my pace to hush it. Fynn walked ahead of me and Kent was practically glued to my back. We made it to the emergency exit sign and I listened to Fynn fumble around in the dark for a door handle.

He found it, and ever so slowly, pushed the door open by about an inch. Then he pressed his face to the crack to get a look at what was outside. "It's a store," he said quietly, "the place looks deserted. Looks like most of the people made it out when shit went down."

"Good," I said, "let's go then."

Fynn pushed the door open and we found ourselves standing in a small retail store. Women's clothing was draped across mannequins and sequins winked at us under the emergency lighting.

"What the hell is this place?" Fynn asked, pinching the glitzy fabric of a blue gown between his thumb and forefinger. "It looks like a night club."

"Prom dresses," I said.

Fynn made a sound in the back of his throat that was half a grunt and half a chuckle. He let go of the dress still pinched between his fingers and we made our way out through the arched doorway and into the hallway of the mall.

The place was deserted. The marble floors were littered with abandoned shopping bags and garbage. There had been a sidewalk sale when it all happened. Stores had tables and racks placed outside their doors with half price signs plastered to metal frames. There were several stains of blood on the floor all the way down the hallway to the other end, which, to my relief, was where we needed to go. "Look," I said, pointing to the doors at the end of the hall.

Above the glass doors was a sign that read 'Station'. Beside the text was a little white photo of a train.

We half ran half jogged across the marble floor. When we reached the door we waited. I pressed my hands to the glass and peered inside. Nothing was moving in there. I could see outlines of benches and glowing signs with destinations flashing on them. I saw Seattle and Lynden and a pang of anxiety hit me.

Fynn opened the doors and we slipped inside.

To our immediate right was the wall of windows that looked out onto the train platform. The irregulars were watching us with their glowing orb eyes. The tall one was listening. I spotted a staff only door that had a picture of stairs on it. "Come on," I said, "we have to get up there. Winston was sure the control room was on the second floor."

The boys followed after me as I raced to the door, wrenched it open, and began running up them. They passed me on the second flight as they took the steps two at a time. We emerged on the second level slightly out of breath and with our heads on a swivel.

A hollow scream from close by nearly made me jump out of my skin. I instinctively grabbed hold of the closest thing to me; naturally, it was Fynn's arm.

An irregular was hurtling towards us. For the first time I was unable to tell if this had been a man or a woman. Everything about its size and shape was average- except for the arms, which seemed unnaturally long as they swayed limply at the irregular's sides.

Kent screamed for us to follow him. We darted after him around a sharp corner. I almost stopped dead in my tracks when I saw what was at the end of the hallway.

Six or more irregulars were all on their knees on the carpeted floor. Someone- a man- was sprawled beneath them. I could see his body jostling as the monsters buried their hands in the dead man's stomach and withdrew fistfuls of guts, which they proceeded to slurp off their fingers or drop directly down their throats. My stomach rolled and I tasted bile at the back of my throat.

I didn't notice that I had stopped running. Fynn grabbed my hand as he blew past me and practically yanked me off my feet. The irregulars that were intent on devouring the man at the end of the hall were getting to their feet. Their pale eyes were fixed on us and their mouths were gaping like fish out of water. Then the screaming started.

Kent ducked to his right and disappeared through an open door. I followed him in, and Fynn came behind me with just enough time to slam the door closed and lock the handle. The two irregulars on the other side began screaming with rage and throwing themselves at the door. It shook on its hinges.

"They'll break through that in no time," I said, looking wildly around.

We were in what appeared to be a security room. It was small, no bigger than my bedroom at home, and one wall consisted of dozens of security monitors. All of them were off.

Kent called us over to something hanging on the wall. He pressed his finger to what I at first thought was just a poster. Upon closer inspection I realized it was a detailed map of the building. Kent ran his finger along a thick white line and stopped above the words 'Control Room'. "We don't have far to go," he said rather confidently, "it's just across the hall from us and six rooms down."

"How do you propose we get out into the hall with those things waiting for us?" Fynn asked dryly, his right eyebrow arching dramatically.

Kent cracked a devious smile. "We go over them."

"Over them?" I asked.

"Yeah, this shows all the ventilation shafts in the building." Kent pointed upwards at a grate in the ceiling. "If we go up and over, we can drop down into the control room. We leave, one by one to distribute our weight throughout the shaft, and drop down outside of the station back in the mall. Somewhere we know is already clear. We go out the same door we came in and make a break for the train."

"I can't think of anything better," Fynn said, dragging one of the chairs tucked under the security desk over beneath the ceiling grate. He stepped up and removed the grate. "Where do I go?"

"Right to cross the hall," Kent said as he peered at the map, "then take another right. You should be able to see through grates like this one in to each room. You'll know when you're above the control room. We'll be right behind you."

It took every ounce of will power I had to refrain from telling them that I was claustrophobic. Giving voice to the fear would only make it worse. So, I followed Fynn up into the shaft and found myself lying flat on my stomach staring at the soles of his boots. They were coated in dark dried blood. He began to crawl forward on his elbows and I followed, trying my best to ignore the impending feeling of being crushed to death by the metal siding. It was only slightly less terrifying than the prospect of being eaten alive.

I heard Kent come up behind me. Our breathing was raspy and not at all quiet as we made our way over the hallway. I didn't look down the grate we passed. I didn't want to see down there and I knew I had the sort of luck that would have placed us right above the half eaten corpse. I didn't need an aerial view of that.

We turned right and continued our military crawl good fifty or so feet. Finally Fynn paused to stare down through one of the vents. "This one," he said quietly. I couldn't see around him in the shaft, so I listened to him remove the vent. It fell loudly to the ground in the control room, and the startled shrieks from below sent waves of relief through me. The people we were risking everything for were still alive. We had made it.

Fynn dropped through the opening and began calling out to the people who had made the call. I jumped down after him. Shocks of pain wove up my ankles from the impact. I limped out of the way for Kent to come down after me.

I hovered behind Fynn's back as he held out an arm in front of me. I drew up to my tip toes to see over his shoulder.

A group of people were huddled on the ground in front of him. They had boxed themselves in by moving several desks into the middle of the room. This confused me until I looked around. The wall to our immediate right was made of etched glass. It wasn't entirely see through, but I could see the shapes of the irregulars outside, who had their mouths pressed against the glass. Their tongues and lips left wet streaks in their wake as they moved up and down, left and right, growling ravenously.

"We heard your distress call," Fynn said, "and we can get you out of here, but we have to move now. Is everyone alright?"

The people in the middle of the ring of desks were normal people. None were employees. There was a middle aged man with graying sandy blond hair. He was getting unsteadily to his feet and wiping his hands anxiously on his thighs. His eyes darted between the three of us before flicking up to the hole in the ceiling. "Will that hold all of us?" He asked.

"One at a time, spaced out, yes. Hopefully," Fynn said.

The man rubbed the back of his head and continued to stare at the hole. Then he nodded as if he had convinced himself. He turned back to the others who were still sitting on the ground. "Let's go," he said.

A woman in a purple skirt and wrists full of bracelets stood next. Behind her cowered two young girls who instantly made me think of Addison. They hid from view behind their mother, whose bracelets jingled like Christmas bells.

"Take those off and leave them," Fynn said to her.

She blinked in surprise.

Fynn opened his mouth to tell her again, but I intervened. I stepped around him and spoke softly. "Some of the things out there have heightened hearing. We don't want to give away our position. We have a way to get everyone out, we just need to be as quiet as possible. Okay?"

The woman pursed her lips and stared at me. Then she pulled the bracelets off and set them down on one of the desks.

The two other people got to their feet. They were a young boy and girl, maybe only eighteen or nineteen. I knew right away that they were a couple. He was wearing a striped polo shirt and had his arm wrapped around her waist. She was pressed against his side in fear. I didn't blame her. The boyfriend tugged at the hem of his polo shirt as he looked over the three of us nervously. "How did you guys get here?"

"Train," Fynn said shortly.

"And you got inside the station? What's it like outside? Is this happening everywhere? Where are the police? How many of you are there-"

"Listen," Fynn said, "I know you have questions, and we'll answer them when we don't have a horde of flesh eating creeps trying to get at us, alright?"

The teenager nodded, somewhat embarrassed, and his girlfriend took his hand in hers. She tucked a loose strand of hair behind her ear. "Thank you for coming to save us."

Fynn faltered under the gratitude. "Uh, yeah, well, it was her idea." He hooked his thumb over his shoulder to point at me.

"Thank you," the girl said again.

I felt my cheeks grow hot. "You're welcome."

Something heavy slammed into the glass wall. I whirled around to see that one of the irregulars had hurled herself into it. A crack had formed in the middle of the glass and was snaking outwards like an ever growing spider web.

"No time for friendly chit chat," Fynn said, "Kent, you get up there and lead the way. We'll send the kids up first,"

Kent nodded and brought a chair under the open vent. He climbed up and swung himself around so that his arms were hanging out of the hole. The man with sandy hair stepped forward with both of his daughters. They were starting to cry. He bent down in front of them and took hold of one of each of their hands.

"These people came to help us," he said, "and we have to be brave right now, okay? We are going to get out of here. Listen to what they say. Don't cry. Keep quiet. Mommy and daddy are right behind you." He kissed their cheeks and lifted one of the girls up under her armpits. Her reaching hands were met by Kent's, who pulled her up into the vent with him. The other girl was quick to follow.

The same irregular hurled herself into the glass again. The crack crept further towards the ceiling and the floor. We didn't have much time.

Kent took the lead down the vent and I could hear the sound of his clothes dragging along the bottom of the shaft as they made their way out of the room and down the side of the hallway. The mother went next, followed by the father.

The young couple stepped up to the chair. The girl was quite pretty despite the mascara that had left tear tracks down her cheeks. She had long black hair that was tied up in a ponytail that swished against her lower back as she clambered up into the vent. Her boyfriend followed. He was a little clumsy and struggled to lift himself up and he tore the hem of his polo shirt on the metal edge of the ventilation shaft. Fynn waited until everyone was making their way down the vent before he nodded for me to get up on the chair.

I put one foot on the seat and he offered me his hand to help me stand. I didn't need the help, but I accepted nonetheless. His hand was warm and softer than I expected. I stepped up on the seat and he loosened his grip, letting his hand fall to his side.

I glanced down at him before I reached up to hoist myself into the vent. His dark eyes were framed with dark skin that hadn't been there yesterday when this whole thing started. He looked tired. I probably did too. Stubble was darkening his jaw and neck.

"Get your ass up there, Violet," Fynn said, "I'm right behind you-"

An explosion of sound assaulted our ears. I instinctively covered my head as glass rained down on the carpeted floor. It wasn't coming from above me. It was from the transparent wall separating us from the irregulars in the hallway.

"Holy shit," Fynn breathed as one of the irregulars stepped through the broken section of wall. It was about two feet wide. The wall had been built in small sections, probably to prevent the whole thing from shattering if some disgruntled employee decided to throw a chair through it or something. In this particular moment, it prevented all of the irregulars from barrelling into the room at once.

I wanted to scream as the first irregular came straight for us. I didn't have time to get up into the vent. Fynn shouted my name and grabbed my hand again. He yanked me off the chair and the two of us half ran, half stumbled around the octagon of desks in the middle of the room in a desperate attempt to put something between us and the beast intent on devouring us.

"There's too many!" I shouted. "They'll have us surrounded-"

"I know!"

Fynn pulled me along beside him as the irregular made its way around the desks. Like most of the others, this one had its head tilted to the side. Our backs were to the windows that overlooked the platform one floor below. I afforded a glance over my shoulder. The train was on the tracks. The irregulars were swarming towards it. I thought of Cassidy for a terrified, panicky moment before Fynn hoisted a chair over his shoulders and threw it through the window.

More glass shattered and cascaded down. The irregulars

down at the train turned to see what was happening. Their pale eyes settled on the chair on the pavement down below and some of them veered off from the larger group near the train to come investigate.

"We gotta go!" Fynn roared, hauling me towards the now open window frame.

"What?"

"Jump," he said, looking over his shoulder as more of the irregulars filed in through the small opening in the wall. "We don't have any other options. Landing... landing is going to hurt. Feet together. Don't lock your knees. Try to roll out of it."

"Fynn, I can't... I can't do this... it's too high... please-"

His hand settled between my shoulder blades and he pushed me forwards with strength that startled me. I grasped at open air in a desperate attempt to grab hold of the window frame to stop myself from falling out of the window. There was nothing to grab, and I found myself falling feet first to the ground below. It rushed up to meet me with sickening speed.

Fynn's words rang in my head as time seemed to slow down. I knew the fall was only seconds long- two or three at most. I pressed my feet together and bent my knees. The shock of the ground beneath my feet expelled a shout of pain from me as I rolled in a half summersault and ended up on my back, staring up at the open window.

Fynn was standing in the opening. I rolled to my side to get out of the way and sat on my knees while my ankles seared with pain. When Fynn didn't land beside me within the next couple of seconds, I looked up, worry and anxiety building in my gut.

"Fynn!" I screamed, forgetting about the irregulars on the platform by the train.

Fynn was dangling out the window. One of the irregulars- a woman with a purple ribbon in her hair- had a hold of the back of his shirt. She was shrieking as she tried to drag him closer.

"Your knife!" I shouted, getting unsteadily to my feet. "Use your knife!"

I watched in horror as Fynn fumbled for the knife tucked

into his belt. The irregular was pulling him closer to her as the others from out in the hall crowded around the opening of the shattered window. They were reaching out for Fynn with bloodied hands and slack jaws. Their bright white eyes were fixed on him the same way a cat might stare at a bird with broken wings.

Fynn's knife flashed as he ripped it free of his belt. He stabbed it into the arm of the irregular holding him. She didn't react. It was as if she didn't feel it at all. He stabbed again, this time more furiously, but to no avail. Her blood sprayed up the side of his face and over his chest. She was dragging him ever closer. His feet were slipping of the ledge. If they went over the ledge together I knew he wouldn't stand a chance of sticking his landing.

A horn blew. I nearly jumped out of my skin. I whirled around to face the train. Steam soared into the air at the engine as it squealed forward on the tracks.

We were being left behind.

The irregulars on the platform had forgotten about Fynn and I as the train began to depart. They ran after it, some of them collapsing behind it on the tracks and being trampled by the others.

I looked back up at Fynn. We weren't going to make it back to the train in time now. Even if we did, we would stand no chance of getting through the horde of irregulars that were following it.

My head suddenly exploded with pain- it was like someone had poured a jar of pins through an opening in my skull and began vigorously shaking me. Stars flashed white behind my eyelids as I leaned forward and pressed my forehead against the pavement in a desperate attempt to make the white hot agony disappear.

And then it did.

I was left feeling empty and numb. My ears were ringing the same way they had the first time I went outside after my first concert as a young girl. As the ringing pitch began to fade another noise was added to the mix. It was soft and low, like a gentle whisper.

When the sound morphed into a voice and began speaking to me, I sat bolt upright. Dizziness set in and my vision swam. I tried to look up at Fynn but the world tilted and spun and I was forced to lean over again.

"You are one of us," the voice hissed in my head, *"you are one of us."* It was a man. His voice sounded wet and raspy, like his throat had been torn out and his lips were soaked in blood and saliva. He repeated the chant, and it echoed in my head like a living migraine.

I was screaming Fynn's name. The voice in my head was getting louder. I pressed my palms against my ears to try to silence it, but I only managed to block out all the other sounds around me, and the husky male voice was amplified in the quietness of it all.

"Don't resist. You are one of us. Come."

"Fynn!" I shrieked, releasing my ears and looking back up at the window despite the wave of dizziness and nausea that crashed over me again.

Above me, Fynn raised his arm with an angry yell and buried his knife in the irregular's skull. Blood sprayed out and stained the ribbon in her hair. Her hand in the front of his shirt released him. Fynn's arms flailed wildly at his sides as he tipped backwards out the window. I held in my scream for him, reminding myself that the irregulars chasing the train had temporarily shifted their focus away from us. I had to make sure it stayed that way.

Fynn's fall felt like it lasted hours. I watched, my stomach giving way to terrified butterflies, as he fell backwards out the window. As he fell to meet the pavement the voice in my head began to subside to a menacing whisper. I shook my head and gritted my teeth to try to chase it away.

Fynn landed with a hard smack with his back to me. Then he rolled on his side and desperately clutched at his left leg.

I pushed myself to my feet and ran to him. I dropped to my knees beside him and ignored the voice that was growing farther and farther away. "Are you okay?"

His eyes were screwed closed and his jaw was clenched. He

pressed his forehead against his knee and made a pained sound in the back of his throat.

"You need to get up," I said, wrapping my hands around his right arm and trying to haul him up beside me, "we don't have time. If we can make it to the trees we can hide. Please Fynn, you have to get up."

He kept his mouth shut as I dragged him upwards. He put his weight on his left leg, crumpled, and fell back to the pavement. "You have to go," he said breathlessly. I could hear the pain in his voice. "Get out of here," he pushed me roughly away.

I stumbled backwards but surged back to his side. I wrapped his arm over my shoulders and lifted him with my legs. He stood on his right leg and looked over at me. I could smell him. Sweat, stale cologne, booze. "We're going together," I said evenly. The words sounded brave. They sounded like I was some sort of hero refusing to leave a fallen soldier behind. The truth was, I was terrified to be alone. I needed someone, and Fynn was the only someone around.

I set my sights on the tree line on the other side of the tracks. It was roughly half a football field away- maybe a bit further. I put one foot in front of the other and Fynn hopped along beside me on his right leg. His left was slightly bent and his foot hovered inches above the pavement as we made our way to the trees.

I afforded a glance back up the window. The irregulars were watching us, but didn't seem too keen on the idea of pursuing us.

"What are they doing?" Fynn asked through clenched teeth.

"Nothing," I breathed, focusing on the distance ahead of us to the forest. "They don't seem to care about us anymore."

Fynn stared at me as I continued to hobble with him half draped over my shoulder. He didn't say anything as we reached the tracks. I jumped down first and turned around to help him. He slid off the edge, bit back the sound of pain that tried to escape him when he landed, and looked at me imploringly. I offered him my shoulder and we hobbled as quietly as we could across the tracks as the irregulars chased the train.

"They're fast," I whispered when we reached the grass on the far side of the tracks. "They're really fucking fast."

We rushed under the cover of the trees and pushed deeper into the forest, stepping over roots and branches to avoid making noise. Fynn was tiring and I knew he needed to rest. I wasn't willing to sit down yet. I wanted to put as much distance as we could between us and the irregulars if they happened to wander back to the platform. I also wanted to make sure we were out of earshot.

When Fynn slid off my shoulder some fifteen minutes later, I dropped down beside him on the mossy forest floor. He collapsed on his back and closed his eyes. One hand was draped across his chest and the other arm was splayed out at his side. His breathing was sharp and his stomach rose and fell quickly.

"Are you okay?" I asked.

He didn't answer right away. Finally he shook his head, opened his eyes, and swallowed. "I think my leg is broken."

"Are you sure?" I asked. "Maybe it's a sprained ankle or something. Maybe the fall was just too much. Maybe it will pass and-"

"Violet," he said, propping himself up on his elbows and fixing me with his dark brown eyes, "it's broken."

I stared at him lamely. A broken leg in this mess... how was he going to get around? How was it going to heal? I closed my eyes and pressed my hand against my forehead. "Shit." A lump rose in my throat. I couldn't cry. Not right now. "We never should have gone in there. If we had stayed on the train none of this would have happened."

"Violet, give me a break. Shit happens."

"Shit like this doesn't just happen!" I said loudly. "People are eating people, Fynn. Everyone is dying. My best friend just left me behind to die. And you're leg is broken. And we're alone. What are we going to do?"

Fynn sat up and rested a hand on my knee. "We keep going. There's nothing else to do. Your sister is waiting for you. Nothing has changed."

I blinked furiously to get rid of the tears that were clinging to my eyelashes. I wiped them away with shaking fingers, took a deep and shaky breath, and met Fynn's dark stare. "You're right."

"I know."

I pushed myself to my feet and looked around. We were enclosed by thick tree trunks. The leaves above provided thick cover from the sun. It would be cool when night fell. "We need to do something about your leg," I said. "Maybe we can make a splint or something- anything to make walking easier until we can find a car or an easier way to get around."

Fynn nodded. "Alright."

The surge of emotion that had broken over me was passing. I focused my attention on the task at hand and pushed aside the heavy feeling of guilt that was following me around as I began searching the forest floor for a straight enough branch to use as a splint.

"Hey, Violet," Fynn said tentatively. I looked up at him as I bent down to investigate a promising looking branch. He looked for a moment like he was going to tell me to forget it. When he spoke I could tell he was picking his words carefully. "When I was up there... on the window... I could hear you screaming."

I didn't want to think about the voice that had consumed my mind. I had managed to suppress the terrifying memory to focus on the more important things at hand. Fynn's question brought a whole new torrent of fear upon me. If I told him he would think I had gone mad. If I didn't say anything I thought I might go crazy anyways. My mouth was suddenly dry.

"Violet," Fynn said again, "what happened down there?"

I took a deep breath, stooped down, and plucked a straight, thick branch off the forest floor. I twirled it end over end in one hand before tucking it under my arm. "I think I went crazy for a minute there."

Fynn blinked.

"I thought you were going to die, and I panicked. I thought I was going to be alone."

Fynn looked away from me. I could see the tightness in the shadow of his jaw. He shifted himself around and winced when he jostled his injured leg.

I joined him on the forest floor, dropping to my knees and holding out the branch I had found. "This is the best I could do."

Darkness was settling in around us and filling the gaps between the trees with inky dark voids. Fynn was leaning back to rest on his elbows and extending his wounded leg out straight in front of him. "I'm going to need your help with this," he said.

"Yeah," I said, "of course."

We didn't have any supplies. There was nothing on hand to tie the branch to his leg. I untied my sweater from around my waist and began tearing the sleeves off from the shoulders. I used them to secure the make shift splint to his ankle and around the middle of his calf. I needed one more piece to tie around his knee. I used the remaining fabric of my sweater and began tying it tightly to his leg.

"I can't believe they left us behind," I said quietly.

"I can."

CHAPTER 6

Walking through the forest with Fynn and his broken leg was no easy feat. My phone had died a couple hours ago. Fynn's had followed suit some fifteen minutes later, leaving us without a way of knowing the time. It also saved me from checking to see if the service returned every half hour or so.

Fynn was stubborn and insisted on walking by himself. I protested but found myself suffering under his offended glare. He had a big ego, that was for sure, and I realized that I was close to damaging it by making him the damsel in distress.

So, after we had been walking for hours, I had to resist the urge to roll my eyes at him when he stumbled over some raised tree roots. He started cursing up a storm as he leaned against the tree trunk for momentary reprieve.

"We'd move faster if you would just let me help you," I said.

"I'm fine," he said through gritted teeth.

I planted my fists on my hips and sighed. "Good. Because we're losing the sun. Soon we'll barely be able to see in front of our own faces. We're in the middle of who the hell knows where. And, to top it all off, we have no food, no water, no-"

"I get it," he growled, pushing himself off the trunk and limping towards me. "Let's keep going. Or we can keep standing around complaining. Up to you."

This time I rolled my eyes. "Oh yeah, because I'm the one holding us up." I let my hands fall to my sides as I turned around and began pushing deeper into the woods. At some point I was hoping they would thin out and we would find ourselves close to civilization again- or at least find something we could use for shelter to sleep. Lying down on the forest floor with deranged cannibals roaming around wasn't all that appealing.

As I walked I listened to Fynn's boots crunch over branches. I could hear him muttering under his breath and I knew each step was causing him pain. I wanted to help, but I didn't know what I could do that he wouldn't meet with angry resistance. It was becoming quite clear that Fynn was a one man operation. Help seemed to be an entirely foreign concept to him.

So I pushed on ahead, trying my best to clear branches out of his way without him noticing. As I walked I had to consciously force myself to think of the task at hand. If I let my mind wander I found myself breaking out in a cold sweat as I remembered the hissing voice in my head from back on the platform. Just thinking about it for more than a couple minutes made the hair on my arms stand to attention. Goose bumps would break out all over my body and I would have to fight the nearly uncontrollable urge to assume the fetal position against a tree and rock back and forth.

Thinking about the voice was dangerous.

I focused my mind on other things. They weren't much better than the voice. I found myself thinking about Cassidy. I wondered what she had done when the train started to leave. Had she fought the others to get them to stay? Had she cried? Had they hurt her in order to shut her up as they left us behind?

The questions hurt.

"Hey," Fynn muttered from behind me, "what's that?"

I looked over my shoulder at him and stopped walking. He came to stand beside me and tugged me a little to the right. He turned my shoulders a bit so that I was facing an opening between two tree trunks. His hand was still resting lightly on my right shoulder. The warmth from his palm was reassuring. Touch in general was reassuring. I wasn't alone.

Through the darkness of the leaves and branches I saw sky;

dark blue, promising sky, speckled with the faintest glimmer of stars.

"Let's go," I breathed.

I said nothing as Fynn kept his hand on my shoulder and we made our way through the dense trees. His grip was light and I knew he was using me to help his balance so he didn't have to put as much weight on his broken leg. It felt good that he was willing to finally let me help.

It took maybe another twenty minutes or so before the trees started thinning out. We approached cautiously, minding where we put each step so we didn't disturb the branches on the forest floor. We knew that keeping quiet was crucial. Some of the irregulars back at the train station had relied on their hearing to hunt their prey. If some of them were out and about here, we would be at a serious disadvantage.

When we finally emerged from the cover of the trees we found ourselves staring down at a cluster of buildings with metal roofs. It was old, and most definitely abandoned. Nature had crept towards it through the grass fields it was surrounded by. Vines were snaking up the sides of some of the infrastructure. A tall cylinder type structure stood tall at the opposite end from us.

"What is this place?" I asked.

"A mill, maybe," Fynn said, his hand falling from my shoulder. "Lumber mill. I don't know. Doesn't look like anybody's here."

He was right. The place was lonely.

"We can probably find a good place to sleep here," I said.

Fynn looked around. He nodded silently and we proceeded forward, our heads on swivels. The darkness of the trees was unsettling as we made our way further away from it. It had worked as a blanket of cover when we were in it. I had felt somewhat protected in the depths of the trees. Now, from the outside looking in, I couldn't help but wonder what other things it was hiding.

More irregulars, perhaps, making their way through the trees with hollow eyes and open mouths.

The mill was surrounded by chain link fence. We found

a spot that was damaged- it looked like someone had driven through it. We stepped over the broken down fence.

A set of tire tracks ran through the dirt from the chain link fence. We followed the disturbed earth deeper into the mill until we arrived at a parked car. It was an SUV that was caked in mud. It looked as if the windshield had been wiped clean with someone's sleeve. Fynn stopped and tested the handle. The door creaked open and stood ajar as he leaned inside.

"I can probably get this thing running," Fynn said, his voice muffled as he bent under the steering column. "I'll need light. In the morning I'll try to get her going."

"And how are you going to do that?" I asked, crossing my arms over my chest and raising a skeptical eyebrow. "You gonna hotwire it?"

Fynn extracted himself from the vehicle and gave me a sheepish smile. "Yeah, I am."

"Oh," I said, my arms falling to my side. "Seriously?"

"Yeah, I've stolen a few cars in my day. It'll be easy." He shuffled forwards, leaving one hand on the hood of the car for as long as he could to support himself. When his hand fell away I saw a pained grimace scatter across his features. I didn't say anything.

We crept farther into the property. The empty buildings felt like they were consuming us. They stood, hollow and silent, and I crossed my arms around my body for comfort. We made our way past a trailer with a sign posted on the door that read 'Management Only'. "Do you think they would have medical supplies in there?" I asked, stopping to stare at the door.

"Maybe," Fynn said, shrugging weakly.

"Stay here," I told him," I'm going to check it out."

"You shouldn't go in there by yourself-"

"Relax," I said, "there's no one here. I'll knock first." I climbed the three rickety wooden steps below the front door. I paused for a moment with my ear pressed against the wood, and then I rapped my knuckles against it and waited. Silence was the only thing on the other side.

To my surprise the door was unlocked. I stepped inside and

let the door hang open behind me. I could barely see anything in the place. I walked around carefully with my arms stretched out in front of me, feeling for anything I might walk into.

I found a desk. I made my way behind it and pulled open the drawers. I felt around, my fingertips settling on a stapler, notepads, pens, and something cylinder-shaped. I withdrew it and felt it more diligently. It was a flashlight. I clicked it on and a beam of white light exploded out of the end.

I grinned at my own cleverness and cast the light over the office. One wall was covered from floor to ceiling in aluminum filing cabinets. There was a round table with six chairs around it, most likely a meeting place for the managers and foremen of the mill. The wall behind me hosted a shelving unit, and at the top right, I spotted a white box with a red cross on it.

"Boo ya," I said to myself. I shuffled to the end of the shelves and had to step on the lowest one to reach the top. I grabbed the medical kit and hopped back down. Then I searched around for anything else we might need.

In the far corner was a mini fridge. I practically leapt across the room to get to it. I dropped to my knees, yanked it open, and stared in awe at the contents.

Eight water bottles. Six beers. Raspberry yogurt mini containers. Processed cheese. I looked around for something I could put it all in. I found a backpack hanging on the back of the door. I ripped it down and loaded everything from the fridge and the medical kit into it. In a cupboard above the fridge I found crackers, granola bars, and an unopened box of chocolate chip cookies. By the time I had the backpack full I was smiling like an idiot.

I re-emerged outside with one of the shoulder straps of the backpack on. I smiled at Fynn sheepishly. "Let's find a place to spend the night. I have a bunch of goodies we can share."

Fynn hopped on his good leg to look around. "I was thinking we could go up there." He was pointing up at the roof of a two story warehouse building.

"Alright, why so high?"

"I'd rather not be on the ground. Buildings like that have

stairwells inside them. We can block them off so nothing can get up to us. We can both sleep without having to worry about something sneaking up on us."

I was suddenly very aware of how heavy my eyes felt. "Alright."

We walked across the grass invaded gravel and found the door into the warehouse. It was unlocked, just like the office door had been. We stepped inside and listened. I used the flashlight to find the stairwell.

The warehouse was full of wood in different steps of being processed. Most were tree trunks cut into two or three inch thick planks. The ceiling was high and hosted metal rafters with chains hanging down from them. Our footsteps echoed throughout the place with each and every step. Anxiety tickled the nape of my neck.

As we got closer to the door to the stairwell the beam from my flashlight swung over an odd piece of wood. I cast the light back to it and stopped walking.

Leaning up against one of the walls was a long piece of smooth wood that had been carved into a staff. I wrapped my hand around it and lifted it from the wall. It was lightweight and almost the same height as I was.

I handed it to Fynn.

He stared at it in his hand for a moment, then his dark eyes rose to meet mine.

"It will help you walk," I told him, "if you keep putting all your weight on it you're just going to make it worse. Maybe..." I paused, looking around again to see if there was anything that might be of use to us.

The beam of light landed on a workbench on the other side of the warehouse. I hurried over and peered down at the collection of items. More knives. I took them and tucked them in my belt.

Under the workbench was a pile of scrap metal. I crouched down and began rummaging through. I sucked in a sharp breath when I sliced the tip of my finger on something sharp. I sucked the blood off and continued sifting through everything until I found what I was looking for: three pieces of rebar, each two feet long.

"Ah ha!" I said victoriously as I got to my feet.

"What do you need rebar for?" Fynn asked skeptically.

"You'll see," I said, tucking them under my arm as I returned to his side and made for the door at the stairwell. I pulled the door open and we stepped inside.

I took one of the pieces of rebar and slid it through the opening of the door handle. If something or someone tried to push the door open they wouldn't be able to get through.

"Smart," Fynn said. I thought I detected a hint of respect in his voice.

"Thank you," I said, my voice muffled behind my hand. "Now let's get up there."

Fynn nodded his agreement and stepped aside for me to lead the way. I shined my flashlight up the first half flight of stairs and we began making our way up. I listened to Fynn's new staff tap each step one at a time. By the time we reached the landing to tackle the second half flight his brow was furrowed. I knew his leg was hurting him.

"No need to rush," I said, trying to be helpful.

He didn't say anything as we continued to make our way upwards. I shined the light down the steps for him so he could see where he was putting his feet, and I waited patiently at each landing for him to join me before I moved up ahead again.

We arrived on the roof a little out of breath. I closed the door behind us and Fynn leaned against it. Pain was evident on his face, and I let him compose himself in peace.

The roof was covered in gravel save for one corner which had been covered with concrete squares. There were three benches, all facing inwards. A small table sat between them and hosted nothing but an ashtray full of old cigarette butts. This must have been a place where some of the workers would come to have a break. I sat down on one of the benches and put the backpack between my legs. I tucked the two pieces of rebar under the bench.

Day Of Awakening - The Beginning

"Fynn, come sit."

I was surprised when he pushed himself off the door and hobbled over to me, using his staff for support. He surprised me again by sitting down beside me. I had expected him to opt for his own bench where he could stretch out his broken leg. He propped the staff up against the back of the bench and draped his arms over the backrest. He tilted his head back and stared up at the starry night sky.

"Smells better up here," he said.

"Yeah, it definitely does. And," I leaned over and unzipped the backpack. I straightened up and rested it on my lap. I gave Fynn a devious smile as I stuck my hand inside the main pouch. I withdrew a bottle of beer and handed it to him. "I found drinks and food."

I put the backpack between us on the bench and Fynn started looking through it. He pulled out the cheese and crackers and laughed up at the sky. "I'm fucking starving," he said, setting to work at unwrapping the cheese.

I grabbed myself a beer as well and then frowned at it. "We don't have a bottle opener."

Fynn tucked his beer between his knees and held out his hand for mine. I gave it to him. He shifted in his seat to pull out his knife and then stared down at the still somewhat bloody blade. "On second thought, let's use yours," he said, looking at the knife against my hip.

I gave it to him and watched as he slid it up the neck of the bottle quickly. The glass shattered and the top burst off. Not one drop of beer fell to the pavement. He handed me back the bottle. "Be careful, it'll cut your lips up pretty good. Just try to pour it into your mouth."

I took my first sip while Fynn cracked his open. He gave me my knife back and we settled back against the bench. Fynn began slapping cheese on the crackers. He handed me one and I took it thankfully.

The first bite was heavenly. I hadn't realized how hungry I was. The summer heat and the fear had chased away the grumbling in my belly a long time ago. I sighed with contentment and helped myself to more food.

"Did you ever think about the end of the world before this?" Fynn asked me suddenly.

I had just jammed a cracker in my mouth. I covered my mouth as I chewed and shook my head. After I swallowed I finally answered him. "No, to be honest, I think I was too worried about pouring shots and making tip money. Did you?"

"Not really."

"Ignorance is bliss, right?"

Fynn smirked and took several mouthfuls of beer. He wiped his mouth with the back of his hand. "Nah. I just never entertained the thought that things could get any worse than what they already were."

I stared at my hands. I had always known that Fynn had had a rougher go of things than most people. Living in such a small town didn't offer much in the sense of privacy. I'd seen him walking around with bruises and a limp on more than one occasion.

He leaned back and clasped his hands behind his head. He straightened his broken leg out in front of him with a couple grimaces.

"Oh," I said, springing to my feet, "I totally forgot I grabbed these for your leg." I crouched down and grabbed the two pieces of rebar I had slid under the bench. I held them up, one in each hand, and waggled them at him. "These will work better than the branch, at the very least."

I shuffled over to kneel beside him. He sat staring at me as I began undoing the strips of fabric I had tied to his leg. "How does it feel?" I asked.

He unclasped his hands from behind his head. "Not great."

I pursed my lips and pulled the branch away. I began rolling up his pant leg. He let me do it without muttering a word. I was worried as to what the extent of the damage would be beneath his jeans. Part of me was expecting to find part of his bone jutting out of his flesh.

I was relieved to discover no such thing. I could tell there was a broken bone because his shin wasn't flush. I didn't know if I was supposed to push it back into place or not. I decided that I probably should.

"This isn't going to feel too good," I warned him.

"Do your worst," he said. I saw his knuckles turn white as he gripped the back of the bench.

I gritted my teeth and pressed my fingers against the part of his shin that was pushing forwards. I let out a deep breath and pushed with all my might. The bone shifted beneath my fingers. Fynn let out a short, pain grunt, and stiffened above me.

"I'm sorry," I said, pushing harder until I felt the bone slide back into place. Fynn was struggling to catch his breath. I didn't want to look at his face and see the pain I had caused him.

I held one piece of rebar to one side of his leg. "Can you hold this in place for me?"

He obliged and leaned forward to hold the rebar against his leg while I rested the second piece against the other side. His fingers brushed mine as he held on to that one as well. I began fastening the pieces of rebar to his leg the same way I had with the branch. I began tying my sleeve around his ankle first.

"You should have been a nurse instead of a bartender," Fynn said, still somewhat out of breath.

I didn't look up at him as I continued working. "My mom used to tell me that all the time. She's a nurse, too. I think that's where I get it from. Whenever I'd hurt myself as a kid she was always so attentive and gentle. She's the same way with Addison."

"Why didn't you go for it?"

"Go for what?"

"Nursing," Fynn said.

"I don't know," I shrugged, "I guess I just got comfortable at the bar. I made decent money. Tips were good. The job was easy. I got a lot of free booze."

"Free booze," Fynn chuckled, "that's how they get you."

I began tying my other sleeve up around his knee. "What about you? What did you do for work before all this?"

"Well, I had a decent paying roofing job. It was the first job I ever had that was worth keeping. My boss was a no nonsense kind of guy. He paid well. He took a risk, hiring my ass. He knew my dad, you see, so I think he had his doubts about me before I ever set foot on one of the job sites."

"But he hired you anyway?"

"Yeah, he was desperate for guys and I was desperate for cash. He asked me why I wanted to work for him, and then, low and behold, he hired me."

"What did you tell him?"

Fynn raised an eyebrow at me.

"What did you tell him when he asked you why you wanted the job?" I stood up and sat back down beside him on the bench.

Fynn adjusted himself a bit and touched his leg tenderly. He tried to bend it slightly, but the metal held his leg in place. A smile tugged the corner of his mouth. It disappeared as quickly as it came. "I told him I needed to get out from under my old man."

"Oh."

"He gave me the job on the spot. I think he pitied me, a bit, Roy- my boss. He was taking a risk hiring me. He started his roofing company with his older brother, John, who died ten years ago or something. The business was his pride and joy and someone like me stood a hell of a good chance at tarnishing his reputation. But he knew I was desperate, and I think he wanted to help. He and my dad went to high school together. He knew the sort of man he was. He knew how angry he was."

I couldn't think of a single thing to say that didn't sound pathetic. So I drank more beer, and Fynn kept talking.

"After three months of working with Roy I had enough money to move out. I rented a place not far down the street from your little bar. You know Joyce Reddings little antique shop?"

"Yeah," I said, nodding.

"She had two units above the shop. She lived in one. The other was a bit run down, and just a studio apartment, but she let me move in. It was the best thing that ever happened to me and she knew it."

"How long ago was this?"

"Two years."

"That's all the time you had away from him?" I was talking about his dad.

Fynn didn't need me to clarify. He knew exactly what I was asking. "Yeah. Two years. Not enough, but better than nothing."

I wanted to ask him what his father used to do to him, but I knew the question was insensitive. Not only that, but I wasn't sure if I actually wanted an answer. Fynn had been someone around town that I never really gave a second of my time to. He was always angry, and usually drunk, and he made me nervous. He had made a lot of people nervous.

"You want to know what he did to me," Fynn stated.

I blinked nervously and shook my head. "I'm not sure if I do."

He nodded in understanding and looked back up at the sky. The stars were winking above us. There wasn't a cloud in the sky. The moon was bright and full above the tree line we had emerged from.

"If you want to tell me," I said finally, "you can."

Fynn looked over at me. He looked younger than I had ever seen him. His eyes were bright and there was a sort of eager tension in him. He wanted to tell me. He needed to tell me- or just tell someone.

"He would come home piss drunk in the middle of the night when I was young. I used to go to bed and hope he wouldn't bother me if I was sleeping, but I got sick of being woken up by his fists or his yelling. So I started waiting up for him. I'd watch old reruns on TV until his headlights pulled into the driveway. Then I'd turn off the TV and sit in the living room and wait for him. He'd come barging in, hell-bent on getting his hands on me. I never fought him. Never tried to get away. He was too strong and fighting back only ever made it worse."

I looked at the beer in my hands and swallowed. Fynn had been living in a nightmare for his entire life. Now the nightmare was bigger. It affected everyone. As he continued talking I reached into the backpack and grabbed us each another beer.

"I remember one time he burned me with his cigar. He told me I deserved it. Told me it would help me remember him when he was gone," Fynn laughed without humor and pulled up the hem of his shirt. He tugged down the waistband of his jeans to show me his left hipbone, which was covered in pale pink circular scars.

"That's terrible," I said quietly, looking from the scars to Fynn's eyes.

"He nearly killed me on more than one occasion. I woke up to him giving me CPR once when I was sixteen."

"Are you serious?"

"He strangled me. I remember, right before I passed out, praying that I wouldn't wake up. How fucked up is that?" His eyes darted to meet mine and it took every ounce of will in my body not to look away. There was sadness in him- a grief I had never seen in someone before.

"I'm sorry, Fynn."

"Don't be," he said rather coldly, "it's no one's fault. Shit like that happens to a lot of kids every day."

"Just because it happens to other people doesn't make it okay that it happened to you."

He stared at me for what felt like ages. Finally he looked away and began drinking the new beer I handed him. "I snapped one day," he said suddenly, "I just lost it. I'd been working with Roy for a few months. I'd had a long day. I was tired. My old man came home looking for a fight... I gave him one he wasn't ready for. Broke his jaw. Busted his nose. I felt it break beneath my knuckles and damn that was satisfying."

I was compelled to say something, but I knew nothing I said would erase what had happened to Fynn and his father. Nothing I said would make any of it better. So I stayed quiet and let him continue talking.

"I haven't spoken to him since that night. I moved out the following week. I avoided all the local places he frequented and started going to your little bar. I was free. I wasn't one of the weak ones anymore. I wasn't the sort who was always going to take the beating and look the other way. I became stronger." He sighed and craned his head back to look up at the sky. "And now here we are, right back on the bottom of the food chain."

"We're not at the bottom of the-"

"No?" Fynn asked, irritation and anger colouring his voice. "These *things*," he snarled, "these irregulars... they're the strong ones now. What they're doing to us..."

I chewed the inside of my cheek nervously as we sat in tense silence. He was right. Of course he was right. I couldn't deny the things he was saying. I had seen it all first hand, just as he had. I knew how fast the tables turned when the irregulars attacked. They were primal. They were powerful.

"They're doing to us what we've been doing to animals, I guess," I said, hoping this might defuse some of Fynn's anger. "Evolution made us the stronger species."

"We've never been stronger, we've only been smarter. If you come face to face with a bear or lion or something, it's going to be a really quick battle."

"They're weaker than us because we're smart enough to use tools," I clarified.

"The irregulars don't use tools."

"No," I admitted.

Thinking of such things served no purpose. For now, the best we could do was keep going.

I patted his good leg and got to my feet. I made my way over to the closest bench and began dragging it closer.

"What are you doing?" Fynn asked.

"Well, I figured you should probably keep your leg elevated. Right?"

Fynn shrugged.

"It's better safe than sorry," I said, "and to be honest, if we're going to sleep up here, I don't want to be that far apart. Call me a baby if you want to, but it's taking everything I have not to have a full blown panic attack right now."

"Closer is good with me," he said.

"Good."

I helped him lift his broken leg up. He rested his heel on the opposite bench as I sat down beside him again. I tucked my beer between my thighs and rested my palms on my legs. "Can I ask you something?"

"Sure."

"Your dad," I said slowly, "was he still in Lynden when it happened? Did you leave him behind?"

I could feel Fynn's eyes on me. I refused to look at him. When he finally answered me I kept my stare fixed straight ahead. "I left him behind."

"Do you regret it?"

"No."

I believed him. "I wouldn't either. People like that… people like that don't deserve a second chance." My own words surprised me with how blunt they were.

Fynn started to laugh. This surprised me even more than my own cruelty. When he had himself under control he straightened up and wiped the corners of his eyes with his thumbs. "You're different than I thought you were, Violet, that's for damn sure."

I crossed my arms and glared mockingly at him. "Oh yeah? You thought you had me all figured out?"

"I thought I did. I was wrong."

I grabbed the last two beers from the backpack and Fynn opened them. More glass rained down on the pavement between us. Foam from the neck of his bottle bubbled up and spilled over his fingers.

"What did you think I was like?" I asked.

Fynn drank greedily and I watched his Adam's apple. When nearly half the bottle was gone he looked me straight in the eye. "I was sure you were nothing but a princess. I thought you were spoiled. I thought you were weak. I thought you and Cassidy were just a couple of giggly young girls who didn't have anything worth worrying about."

"I am those things," I said quietly.

"No," he said, "you were those things. Now... now you're kind of a badass. And it looks good on you."

"A badass?" I giggled. "Right. Me. A badass."

"No seriously," Fynn said, finishing his beer and tossing the bottle over his shoulder. It shattered somewhere behind us. "You have balls, Violet. You wanted to save those people at the station. You want to save your mother and your sister, and you're willing to do whatever it takes to get to them. You're risking your life now by hanging around a guy with a broken leg, who's going to do nothing but slow you down. So yeah. You're a badass."

His words floated around in my brain for a while and I realized that I was a little tipsy. Even though I worked in a bar I wasn't much of a drinker. After nearly a day with no food and barely any water, the beer was making short work of my defenses. I licked my slowly numbing lips. "Thanks."

"Thanks?" Fynn chuckled.

"I'm flattered, actually. I never thought I would be someone like this. I always wondered if I was the fight or flight kind of person. It feels kind of good to know I'm the former. You know?"

"Yeah, I do."

As he stared at me, I realized again how dangerously good looking Fynn was. His dark eyes looked nearly black in the moonlight. His jaw was dark with stubble and shadowed in the night. I liked the way he had his arm lazily draped over the back of the bench. I liked the way some of his midriff was peeking out from beneath his shirt. I liked a lot of things about him.

"You alright?" He asked, leaning forward and peering at me curiously.

"Oh. Yes," I stammered, "sorry."

"You're sure?"

All the fear and anger that I had been successfully managing reared its ugly head. I felt suddenly overwhelmed. I was incapable of speech as my hands started to tremble. I looked away from Fynn to hide my face as my eyes grew wet and my bottom lip quivered.

"If you need to cry, now is the time," Fynn said gently.

So I cried. It happened at first in big sobs that left me desperate for air. Fynn rested his hand on my back as I let the emotion pour out of me. As I cried I revelled in the relief of feeling lighter- of feeling like some of the weight I had been carrying around with me was evaporating.

It took me a couple minutes to compose myself. Even when I had got the crying under control I was still a sniffling, misty eyed disaster. I turned back to Fynn, knowing my eyes were puffy and my nose was pink, and forced myself to smile at him. "Thank you for not making it weird."

Fynn chuckled. "What's weird about crying on a rooftop in the middle of nowhere because people have started eating each other?"

I nudged his shoulder playfully. "You can cry too, if you want," I joked.

Fynn grinned sheepishly and shook his head. "Nah. I'm good. But if I need to, I know where to come." He spread his arms out wide as if to embrace the scenery from up on the roof.

"Do you think they're okay?" I asked, bringing my knees to my chest and resting my cheek on them.

"The others?"

"Yeah. I mean... they had to have left us for a pretty good reason, right? Cassidy wouldn't have just let them leave us behind. She would have tried to get them to stay."

"I don't know what would have happened to make them leave," Fynn said, all the lightness in his tone gone, "but the fact is that they did. I don't plan on forgiving them. Do you?"

"It depends."

"On what?"

"On what their reason was. That's why I'm asking."

"The only good enough reason they could have had was if their lives were in jeopardy. But they were safe on the train. Instead of seeing if we could make it to them they made the decision for us. It's over. It's just you and me."

I resisted the urge to cry again. "Yeah. I know."

"We can still get to Seattle. I'm sure of it. We weren't far away when we were back at the station. We can still get you to your mom and your sister."

"Even if we get there," I whispered, fresh tears tickling the corners of my eyes, "what if there's nothing left?"

Fynn's jaw tightened as he stared at me.

"I don't see how all of this couldn't have reached the city. I don't see how they could have been prepared. We might be walking into a war zone... the irregulars might be everywhere- my mother, Addison-"

"Violet," Fynn said, twisting around on the bench so that he was facing me directly, "we don't know what Seattle is going to be. But we have to try. Right?"

I blinked away the tears that blurred my vision and ignored them as they raced down my cheeks. Fynn gathered my hands in his and squeezed them reassuringly.

"We have to try," he said again, this time more firmly. "Once we get there we will at least know for sure."

"Know for sure," I said softly.

"Yes," he said, "and if your mother is anything like you, she'll be holed up somewhere safe with your little sister. You have to stay strong for them. Can you do that? If I can get that car started we can be there as early as tomorrow morning."

Fynn released my hands and I wiped my tears away. After several moments of sniffling and chin trembling, I nodded. "I can do that."

We sat quietly together for some time. After a while the burning in my throat went away, and so did the temptation to cry. It was replaced with crippling fatigue that made it nearly impossible to keep my eyes open. But it was pleasant, sitting there quietly with Fynn, listening to him breathe as the other sounds of the night surrounded us.

Somewhere nearby an owl hooted softly. Crickets were singing far away, filling the night with soft music. I was sure we would wake to the sound of chirping birds when the sun returned.

"You can lay down," Fynn said quietly, draping both his arms over the bench once more. One arm grazed my shoulders as it rested behind me. "I think I'm going to sleep like this. It's comfortable for my leg."

I blinked wearily at him and rubbed my eyes with the heels of my hands. "Yeah. Okay." I shifted around to curl up beside him with my head at the other end.

"If it's more comfortable you can use my leg as a pillow," he offered.

My tongue felt useless in my mouth again. I twisted back around and perched myself awkwardly on the edge of the bench. I looked back at him over my shoulder. "That won't be uncomfortable for you?"

"Nah. It's fine. I'm going to sleep like a baby." He patted his leg teasingly and gave me a crooked smile. "Come on, it's better than a wooden bench."

My fingers curled up under the edge of the bench. He was still smiling at me. I admired the dimples in his cheeks. He ran a hand mindlessly through his hair and the teenage girl in me swooned.

I turned myself around and brought my legs up on to the bench. I lowered myself backwards until my head hit his thigh. I felt my cheeks burn with warmth. I looked up at Fynn to find him staring down at me. The starry night sky was a beautiful backdrop to his handsome face.

"Don't hate me for saying this," he said, "but I'm glad you were the one who was left behind with me."

My cheeks burned hotter. I licked my lips and didn't fight the smile that emerged. "I don't hate you."

"Good," he said, his voice so soft and so quiet I could barely hear him.

Then he leaned over. The leather of his belt groaned. The bench beneath us creaked. The night sky was swallowed by him as he lowered his face to mine. I could smell the beer on his breath.

My eyes closed when his lips touched mine. The kiss was soft and sweet and left me feeling like a pile of pudding on the bench beneath him. His hand cupped my cheek and I found myself becoming breathless at his touch.

My lips parted and so did his, and we explored each other with our tongues. He tasted like beer, too. His hand lowered from my cheek to my neck, where his thumb traced my jaw until he buried his fingers in my hair behind my ear. For a moment, everything felt whole again.

Then the kiss ended, and Fynn straightened above me. His hand found mine and our fingers wrapped around one another's. We stayed like that, basking in the quietness of the rooftop and the endorphins from our kiss.

I stared up at him for as long as I could keep my eyes open. His head was tilted back as he stared up at the sky. I wanted to kiss him again. I wanted to climb up on his lap and show him how truly glad I was that I was not alone.

But I was tired, and he was hurting, and sleep was just as appealing as another kiss.

CHAPTER 7

My face was warm and everything behind my eyelids seemed to be glowing. I opened my eyes to find myself staring up into blinding light. I pressed my hand to my forehead and used it as a visor before sitting up, throwing my legs over the side of the bench, and peering around the roof.

I was alone. The sun was casting everything into such a stark brightness that I couldn't look at anything white. I kept my eyes down as I stood and stretched, then shuffled over to the ledge of the roof to look around.

I spotted Fynn's legs dangling out the driver's side door of the SUV down below. He had woke me up when the sun first rose and told me he was going to go down and try to get it started. I opted to stay on the roof for a little longer. I hadn't intended on falling back asleep, but the time alone was peaceful and I felt more refreshed now than I had earlier.

I heard the engine of the SUV turn over a couple of times before roaring to life. Dark smoke bloomed out of the exhaust like an angry smoke creature and crept upwards. I watched as Fynn threw the backpack I had filled the previous night before into the back seat. He slammed the door, hobbled around the hood, and climbed into the passenger seat. I could see him recline the seat through the windshield. He knotted his hands behind his head. He was too far away for me to tell, but I was sure his eyes were closed.

My lips tingled as I thought about the kiss we shared last night. I pressed my fingertips to them and closed my eyes. I still couldn't believe that I had kissed him. Forty eight hours ago I hated his guts- forty eight hours ago the world was a different place.

I sighed and opened my eyes again, scanning the abandoned mill and dense line of trees surrounding the property. Birds were chirping happily and occasionally taking flight, bursting out of the leaves in a flurry of feathers and song. It seemed as though none of the horrors of the previous day had even happened. Here, everything was serene and untouched. Here, I was surrounded by the illusion of safety.

My eyes drew back to Fynn. I was about to go and spend time alone with him in a car. Under different circumstances I would have looked forward to a mini road trip in the middle of the summer with a boy I had just kissed- a boy with rugged good looks and a scowl that, for some reason, made my knees feel like pudding.

But it had only been one kiss, and I was the only girl around for him to choose from. Maybe he didn't have the same stirrings that I had. Maybe the beer just chased away the need to be... reserved. The kiss had been a sweet surrender from all the stress we had been under. At least, it had been for me. For Fynn it could have been something else entirely.

It could have been nothing.

I sighed and tucked my hands under my armpits. There were more important things to concern my thoughts with besides kissing Lynden's biggest rebel; like finding my mother and sister, for one. My mind was still consumed with thoughts of Cassidy. I wondered if the train had made it to Seattle, and if it had, what had they found? I hoped she was alright. I hoped she hadn't been part of the decision to leave Fynn and I behind.

I practically jumped out of my skin when the horn on the SUV blew down below. Birds shrieked with surprise in the trees across from me and scattered in the sky. I waved down at Fynn, unsure if he could even see me, to try to tell him I'd be down in a minute.

I turned from the ledge and crossed the gravel to the door,

where I let myself into the stairwell and fumbled down the flights of stairs in almost complete darkness. I had told Fynn to take the flashlight with him when he went down- he needed it more than I did with his broken leg.

When I finally made it to the ground level I was relieved to step out into the light of the warehouse. My sneakers squeaked on the concrete as I hurried for the door. I let myself back out into the sunlight and crossed the short distance to the SUV.

I yanked open the driver's side door and slid in.

Fynn rolled his head to look lazily at me. "What were you doing up there for so long?"

"I kind of fell asleep," I confessed with a small shrug, "and then I was just enjoying the sun. It was nice up there." I scrunched my nose as the distinct smell of mold reached my nose. "Good God, what is that?"

Fynn smirked as he crossed his hands behind his head again. "Couldn't tell you. Reminds me of the time I left a cup of milk in my room for a few weeks, though."

"That's disgusting."

This time Fynn shrugged. "Yeah well, it's the only car to pick from. It could be worse."

I put the vehicle in drive and took my foot off the break. We slowly made our way off the property and towards the opening in the chain link fence we had entered through. Once we were on the outside I drove around to a clearing in the trees Fynn directed me to. A dirt road led through them. About a quarter mile up the road there was a crooked old sign that read 'Highway, 3.5 miles'. Once we made it out on to the highway it would be a straight shot to Seattle. I had driven there dozens of times to visit my mother over the last few months, and once I was on familiar pavement, I know I would be able to get us there.

I punched the buttons on the dash to try to turn the radio on. Each and every station flooded the speakers with static. I groaned with exasperation and leaned back in my seat.

"What did you expect?" Fynn asked.

I decided not to answer him. I had been hoping to hear

voices. Preferably they would be voices from people who could tell us what was going on in the world. I had hoped a reporter would be on the air promising safety in Seattle. I had hoped for anything.

The dirt road eventually widened into a gravel one, which in turn become smooth asphalt. We drove through open fields of wheat and grass until, to my sheer delight, we found a connector to the highway.

The highway was deserted. We passed a sign that told us Seattle was in twenty more miles. Three miles later we drove through a section of highway that was littered with abandoned vehicles. I had to slow down to weave through them. We kept our eyes peeled for people who may have stayed behind, but saw no one. The silence in the car was deafening.

"I don't like the look of this," I muttered as I guided the car between two abandoned mini vans.

Fynn was leaning forward in his seat with one hand wrapped around his seatbelt. His eyes were narrowed as he peered through car windows and down the highway. I wasn't sure what he was looking for. Maybe he had been hoping we would come upon some people too.

"Me neither," he admitted, leaning back and resting his elbow on the lip of the window. He glanced at the dashboard. "Better not slow down too much, we barely have enough fuel to get us the rest of the way."

The needle was hovering just above empty. I gripped the steering wheel tighter as we left the cluster of cars in the rear view mirror. I turned the crank to roll my window down. Warm summer air blew through the car and muted the terrible smell of mold. Now it smelled like grass and hot pavement.

We passed another sign. Seattle was only ten miles away.

"Are you nervous?" Fynn asked, his eyes darting to my white knuckles as my grip on the steering wheel tightened even more.

"Yes," I said, without taking my eyes off the road.

"You never know what we might find there," he said,

"maybe the city is untouched. Maybe we'll be the ones to warn them what's coming."

His words were intended to be reassuring. I was sure of it. But they didn't ease the nagging worry in my gut. "If the city is untouched why did we just pass abandon cars?"

I could feel Fynn staring at me as I kept my eyes fixed on the road. Out of my peripheral I saw him turn his chin towards the window. "It doesn't look good," he admitted quietly.

My eyes started to sting and my throat ached. I stretched my fingers and pressed the heels of my hands against the wheel before gripping it again. Fynn remained silent as I struggled to keep my emotions in check. We would be there within another fifteen minutes. Maybe less. There was no point in crying now. I would know for sure soon enough.

We rounded a bend in the highway that turned into an overpass. On the right, outside Fynn's window, buildings suddenly reached for the sky. I swallowed and took a shaky breath. There were still no cars on the highway even though we were just outside the city limits.

Fynn had his nose practically crushed up against the window as he peered down over the overpass to try to get a good look at the streets below. "I don't see any people," he said, "maybe that's a good sign? Maybe the city was evacuated?"

"Maybe," I said, feeling a little bit of hope at his words. It hadn't occurred to me that there might have been an evacuation order. I pressed my foot down heavier on the gas pedal. The engine roared and chattered and more smoke billowed out behind the vehicle as we came down the overpass and I took the exit into the city.

We wove down through a tunnel a couple minutes later. "This lets out in the city," I told Fynn, my heart starting to pitter-patter chaotically in my chest.

"Right," he said, and I could hear the nervousness in his voice. I glanced over at him. His face was pale and his eyes were glazed over as he looked out the windshield.

I reached over and grabbed his hand that was resting on his

knee. His fingers curled around mine and gave them a reassuring squeeze.

"Whatever happens up there," Fynn said, "we'll get through it. Alright?"

I nodded as my eyes began to burn again. "Alright."

Maybe our kiss had meant the same thing to him as it had to me, after all.

Light filled the tunnel as we approached the exit. My mouth was dry and my hands were sweaty. Fynn didn't seem to care. My left knee was bouncing with nerves and I was gnawing the inside of my cheek so forcefully that I could taste my own blood on my tongue.

We emerged from the tunnel and were forced to flip down our visors against the glare of the sun. We drove up a winding curved road which widened into one of the main streets on the city.

We were flanked by office towers on both sides. Little shops and cafes filled the bottom levels and I watched the reflection of our SUV pass through the windows.

"Watch out!" Fynn shouted, leaning sideways and grabbing hold of the steering wheel. He gave it a quick jerk and we narrowly missed slamming into the back of a moving truck that was stationary in the middle of the road.

I slammed the breaks and the tires shrieked on the pavement until we drew to an abrupt stop. "Sorry," I breathed, glancing back over my shoulder at the moving truck.

Both of the doors were hanging open. The hood was crumpled and the windshield was smashed… and stained with a red wetness.

I turned around to peer out our windshield.

My stomach rolled over. I couldn't breathe. I was acutely aware of my own heartbeat and my pulse fluttering at my neck and wrists. Fynn was breathing loudly beside me. His grip on my hand had tightened to the point where it was almost painful. My knuckles were crushed up against each other, but I didn't say a word. I continued to stare dead ahead at the intersection before us.

Cars were scattered all over the place like a giant had swept through the city and used them as toys. Some were burning, sending columns of smoke and flame up into the air. Bodies were plastered on the street in states of such gore that I thought I might throw up. There was so much blood. So much blood.

The lights at the intersection were out. I looked left, down the street, so see only more destruction; a turned over ambulance, a burning five story office building, four abandoned police cars, and, about two hundred feet down the road, there was a young man. He was standing in the middle of the street. He was dressed plainly; blue jeans and a plaid shirt. He was standing nearly right in front of the burning building. The heat from the fire made him look like he was made of gas. He bent and contorted in the heatwaves, but it didn't seem to bother him in the slightest.

"Fynn," I whispered, pointing out my window at the young man.

He spotted him too.

"What do we do?" I asked.

The man was still motionless. His mouth was open. Fynn and I both knew what he was. He wasn't human- not anymore. He had changed, like all the others.

Fynn leaned across my lap and locked my door for me. He proceeded to lock his own, and then he awkwardly reached into the back seats and locked the two back doors, grimacing all the while at the strain he was putting on his broken leg.

"Drive," he said.

"Where?"

Fynn looked at me. His dark eyes were hard, his jaw was clenched, and the anger in him matched the intensity of the sorrow in me. The city was lost. Everything was lost. My eyes burned again, this time more fiercely, and fresh hot tears made their way down my cheeks.

"Do you know the way to the hospital?" Fynn asked.

I blinked and wiped away some of the tears. I nodded, unable to form words over the lump in my throat.

"Take us there," he said, "we've come this far. Don't you want to be sure?"

My mom. Addison. Yes, I needed to be sure.

I looked back the man in plaid on the street. He didn't seem too interested in us- maybe we were too far away for him to see past the fumes of the fire. Even from this distance, I could feel his empty white eyes searching the streets for something to devour.

I swallowed. I had to find my sister. I couldn't let her become one of the irregulars. The thought of her ending up like the man on the road made my chest ache. I rolled my shoulders and set my eyes back on the road as my foot came off the brake. I accelerated slowly so I didn't draw attention to us.

"The hospital is in the downtown core," I told Fynn, "it will be even worse there than it is here."

"Yeah," he said, "I know."

"We'll need a new car at some point. We're almost out of fuel."

"We'll worry about it when the time comes. As long as we can find a safe place I can hotwire another car. For now we just have to get to the hospital."

I nodded more to myself than to him, as if to reassure myself that this was a good idea- that we had a chance in succeeding.

Maybe we did have a chance. Hospitals were safe places with good security. I had to trust that the people there knew what to do in an emergency.

I had to trust that my mom knew what to do to stay alive and get to my sister.

I accelerated faster and the engine roared. Fynn grabbed hold of the handle in the door to steady himself as the SUV rumbled over debris. The vehicle shuddered and rocked and the continuous stream of smoke followed our wake down the deserted city streets.

Fynn was right. We had come too far to turn tail and run now. This was it.

Made in the USA
Monee, IL
19 March 2020